# MAIL ORDER MASSACRE

# More Chilling Reads from Hunter Shea

# MAIL ORDER MASSACRE

*Three Novellas of Pure Terror*

## Hunter Shea

**LYRICAL UNDERGROUND**
Kensington Publishing Corp.
www.kensingtonbooks.com

Lyrical Underground books are published by
Kensington Publishing Corp. 119 West 40th Street New York, NY 10018

All Kensington titles, imprints, and distributed lines are available at special
quantity discounts for bulk purchases for sales promotion, premiums, fund-
raising, and educational or institutional use.

To the extent that the image or images on the cover of this book depict a
person or persons, such person or persons are merely models, and are not
intended to portray any character or characters featured in the book.

Special book excerpts or customized printings can also be created to fit
specific needs. For details, write or phone the office of the Kensington
Special Sales Manager:
Kensington Publishing Corp.
119 West 40th Street
New York, NY 10018
Attn. Special Sales Department. Phone: 1-800-221-2647.

Kensington and the K logo Reg. U.S. Pat. & TM Off.
LYRICAL PRESS Reg. U.S. Pat. & TM Off.
Lyrical Press and the L logo are trademarks of Kensington Publishing Corp.

First Electronic Edition: March 2018
eISBN-13: 978-1-5161-0914-2
eISBN-10: 1-5161-0914-7

First Print Edition: March 2018
ISBN-13: 978-1-5161-0915-9
ISBN-10: 1-5161-0915-5

Printed in the United States of America

# MAIL ORDER MASSACRES

*Three Novellas of Pure Terror*

Just Add Water

Optical Delusion

Money Back Guarantee

# Just Add Water

*For my sea serpents, Star and Samantha*

# Chapter One

*Tuckerville, NY, 1980*

When everything was said and done and the dead were long buried, they would blame Wonder Woman.

While everyone else collected *Star Wars* (the red, yellow, blue and green series) and baseball cards, Patrick Richards and David Estrada plunked every hard-earned nickel they had on comic books. Oh, and there were also the protective plastic bags they had to buy to keep each issue as pristine as possible.

Their habit was expensive, but the thirteen-year-old best friends found ways to scrape together enough money every month to buy the latest issues of *The Fantastic Four, Captain America, The Flash, Marvel Two-In-One* (featuring The Thing and a different guest hero each issue), *Green Arrow* and too many others to count. Well, they could count them. In fact, each could rattle off the total number of comics in their collections at a moment's notice.

"Three hundred and twenty-five," Patrick would say.

"Four hundred and two," David would say, showing off just a bit.

Patrick had a paper route while David mowed lawns for the older people in the neighborhood. Sometimes, they would wait outside the Shopwell supermarket, offering to load people's bags into their cars for tips. An afternoon at Shopwell could net them enough scratch to buy four or more comics.

And there was always shoveling to be done in the winter, along with raking leaves in the fall.

When you had a comic addiction, you had to find ways to feed the beast.

They found themselves in late May flush with cash, thanks to a visit from Patrick's grandparents. His grandfather had slipped a twenty-dollar bill into Patrick's pocket, whispering in his ear, "Don't tell your parents. That's comic book money. Get enough to last the summer."

"You're really gonna share?" David said, staring at the twenty on the floor between them.

"It's not like we don't read the same comics," Patrick said. "The deal is, I get to add more to my collection. Say we split it seventy–thirty?"

David smiled. "I'll take it."

They shook and it was done.

The four-block ride to Blackburn's stationery store had them both in a sweat. Summer had come early. There wasn't a cloud in the sky and the sun was downright brutal. Popping tandem wheelies, they leaped off their bikes at the entrance, both riderless Huffys crashing to the ground in a tangle of metal and rubber.

Blackburn's kept the comics in a long rectangular box on the floor under the magazine rack. The boys got on their knees, carefully rifling through the upright stack.

"We have everything," David said, deflating. His short-cut black hair glistened with drops of sweat.

"Almost," Patrick said, plucking a *Wonder Woman* free. His own face was flushed, bringing the cluster of freckles on his cheeks to blazing prominence.

David considered it, then shrugged his shoulders.

"It's better than nothing."

They paid forty cents for the issue, getting a ton of change that somehow made it seem like they had more money than when they had started. The boys jumped back on their bikes and pedaled home, anxious to get back to David's room because it had an air conditioner.

David read along with Patrick, just over his shoulder. Neither was a *Wonder Woman* aficionado, but neither could argue against the fact that she had one sexy bod.

Sexy for a comic book character. Not as hot as, say, Mrs. Pendleton, freshly divorced and constantly on the prowl. The boys appreciated how difficult she made it for any straight male to not stare at her bulging rack or curvy hips.

They were done in five minutes, the air from the AC making the pages of the comic flutter.

"Well, that was exciting," David said, rolling onto his back.

"It would have made more sense if we had read the previous two issues." Patrick flipped through it again. They'd decided they weren't going to preserve this one. *Wonder Woman* just didn't make the cut for the special-bag treatment.

He perused the endless ads for gag gifts, magic kits, body building guides and footlockers filled with a thousand army men.

His eyes paused on the all too familiar ad for the Amazing Sea Serpents! In the ad, a smiling family of creatures that looked like a cross between mermaids and anacondas, with almost human faces, waved back at him from the comfort of their underwater city.

*Sea serpents make the ultimate pet! No mess! Low maintenance! Just add water and let the fun begin!*

Patrick had always wanted to order the Amazing Sea Serpents, but his parents absolutely forbid him from, in their words, wasting his money on worthless junk.

"All that stuff is a scam," his father had once said. "When I was a kid, I ordered what was supposed to be a working rocket that could break the atmosphere. What I got was a balsa wood stick and a big rubber band."

But that was then, in the old days.

There were laws and stuff now about scams like that. If it was in a comic book, it had to be tested and approved. Stan Lee would never pull one over their eyes. Excelsior!

"We should order the Amazing Sea Serpents," Patrick said.

David had his eyes closed, his hands clasped behind his head. "Huh?"

"They only cost $4.95. You get the serpents, their tank and everything."

Now David sat up. He'd wanted his own for a long time, too, but his parents felt the same way about the whole business as Patrick's.

"We have the money," Patrick said. "And even after that, we'll still have fourteen bucks for the new comics when they come in."

"What about our parents?"

"We don't have to tell them. It says it takes six weeks for delivery. It'll be summer vacation by then. My mom and dad will be at work by eight every morning. I'll be the only one home when the serpents come in the mail. We can set them up in your basement."

David's basement had been a downstairs apartment until the tenants had moved out months earlier. Until his family found new ones, the place was all theirs. Most of the time, they just read comics on the overstuffed couch that had been left behind, eating from brown bags filled with chewy Swedish fish.

"I'll get an envelope," David said, running to the dining room.

Patrick found a pair of scissors and cut the ad out. He would never take scissors to *X-Men* or *Spider-Man*.

At least this way, *Wonder Woman* was serving a noble purpose.

He filled out the order form and David sealed it in the envelope along with a five-dollar bill, licking the stamp. They were going to be out a nickel, but what did it matter?

"I can't wait to see what they look like," David said, a grin splitting his face in half. "I bet they won't be boring as all those beta fish we've had."

On his way home up the street, Patrick dropped it in the mailbox.

Six weeks couldn't come fast enough.

# Chapter Two

Nothing was better than the first day of summer vacation.

Nothing, that is, until Patrick checked the mail and saw the box with a return address from the Bakura Corporation. That's where the Amazing Sea Serpents came from. It took all his will power not to tear the box open. But he'd promised to wait to do it with David.

The box was awful small.

In the ad, it looked like the Amazing Sea Serpents lived in this huge tank surrounded by a veritable underwater metropolis. Whatever was in the box would barely be enough room for a baby hamster to bop around.

Patrick changed quickly out of his school clothes and ran a brush over his teeth. He sprinted to David's house with the box under his arm.

"David!" he shouted through the screen door.

"Oh hey, Patrick," David's mother said, stepping into the hallway. "Come in. David's in his room."

"Thanks, Mrs. Estrada."

"You want something for breakfast? I just made pancakes."

"That's okay. I just ate three cinnamon Pop-Tarts."

He didn't bother knocking on the door. David was sound asleep in his room. It was as cold as a walk-in freezer.

"Wake up, lazy ass."

One eye popped open.

"What the heck are you doing in my room?"

"Look what I got in the mail just now." He held the box over his face.

David rubbed his eyes and sat up. "Oh damn! I almost forgot about them."

"Come on, get dressed so we can put it all together."

They set up shop in the kitchen of the downstairs apartment. Taking turns tearing the brown wrapper and slicing open the box, they carefully extracted the diminutive, oblong plastic tank. Inside it were two packets and a bottle that looked like something eyedrops would come in.

There was a small radio on the windowsill. Patrick turned it on while he shook the box. A folded-up paper landed in his palm. Christopher Cross's "Sailing" came drifting through the lone speaker.

"Nope," David said, turning the dial until he hit on "Call Me" by Blondie.

"All the directions are in Chinese or something," Patrick said, unfolding the square of onionskin paper.

"We don't need 'em," David said. "The steps are written on the bottle and packets."

The bottle was the water conditioner. David read the superfine print on the back of it.

"It says you have to fill the sea serpent home with tepid water."

Patrick's eyebrow shot up. "What the heck is tepid water?"

"It can't mean hot. Or cold. Wouldn't that kill the sea serpents?"

"Maybe it's a special kind of water. You ever see tepid water at the store?"

David turned on the faucet. "We'll just add room temperature water. It works for regular fish."

"If you say so. You better not kill them before they've had a chance to hatch or grow or whatever they do."

Patrick pinched one of the packets between his thumb and forefinger. It said: AMAZING SEA SERPENTS!

"How the heck can sea serpents be in here?" He shook the packet. It sounded as if it were filled with pepper.

"They're supposed to grow when they hit the water, bozak," David replied. He had the water all the way to the fill line. "Now, I have to add three drops to the water and we wait ten minutes."

The other packet was labeled: FOOD.

There didn't seem to be much of it. If these things were going to grow to look like they did in the comics, surely they'd need more than that.

Patrick was beginning to feel that his parents were right.

When it was time to open the sea serpent pack, he was dubious at best.

"What the hell?" David said as Patrick emptied the contents—tiny granules that looked like dark sand pebbles—into the tank. They floated for a moment, then sank lazily to the bottom.

"Well, there goes the serpent dust," David said.

"There's no way those things are gonna grow into sea serpents."

"They look more like fish *food*, not fish."

Patrick read the food packet, opening a corner and spilling some into the palm of his hand. The red flakes, each so small it could fit in the groove of a fingerprint, smelled like low tide at Orchard Beach.

"It says we don't feed them until they've had a week to grow."

David pinched his nose. "That reeks! Wash your hands, man. I don't think we're gonna have anything in a week to feed."

Patrick scrubbed his hands clean.

The boys knelt close to the tank, watching the little black balls sit motionless.

"You think we got ripped off?" Patrick said.

"I don't know. I hope not. Look, we'll just leave them here and check on them every day. Maybe they'll surprise us."

"And where's the city they're supposed to live in? I thought we'd at least get some little buildings and stuff."

David chuckled. "Maybe once they grow, they'll build it themselves. Come on, let's go see if Mike will let us in his pool."

The Amazing Sea Serpents were left on the drain board, but were never far from their minds.

# Chapter Three

To their amazement, life did spring from the packet of serpent dust.

It just wasn't anywhere near what they thought it would be.

Within five days, there were half a dozen wriggling, gray spermy things swimming about. They were a far cry from the smiling Amazing Sea Serpents in the comics.

"Maybe they'll get a lot bigger once we start feeding them," Patrick said, amazed but disappointed.

"Let's just feed them now."

"It said we have to wait seven days."

David unfolded the corner of the food packet and sprinkled half in the tank. The rank odor made them both back away.

"There, now let's see how fast they grow," he said.

"I hope they smell better when they're bigger," Patrick said.

The fledgling sea serpents didn't rise to the top to get at the food. They just kept pulsating in the water, ignorant to the bounty above them.

"I guess those are all dead ones," Patrick said, pointing to all of the black balls of sludge at the bottom. Oddly enough, the dead ones were bigger than the living specks.

"Or maybe they're sea serpent shit. Get one on your finger and smell it."

"*You* sniff sea serpent shit."

"No freaking way. If it smells as bad as the food, I'll throw up," David said.

"If it smells as bad as your farts, I'll throw up, too."

Baseball camp started for the boys and it was five days before they checked on the sea serpents again.

The second they entered the kitchen, they stopped dead in their Keds. Patrick waved at the air. "Whoa, it smells like your mother's cabbage."

"Or a dead mouse. Jeez."

The closer they got to the sea serpent tank, the more they realized exactly where the stench was coming from.

"Well, that's interesting," David said. He picked the tank up, bringing it close to his face while pinching his nose shut. Some of the water had evaporated. It was getting so murky, they could barely see the living sea serpents.

"Only three left," Patrick said. "And they're the same size as they were last week. I can't believe our parents were right."

"Yeah, but look at this." David pointed to the bottom of the serpent tank. It was filled with the black sludge balls. They had tripled in size. "Their shit keeps growing!"

"They're just absorbing the water. ...I think." Patrick tucked the collar of his shirt over his nose to filter out the heady sea serpent aroma.

"We gotta get these things out of here. If my mother or father come down here and smell this, they're going to kill me."

"Should we flush them?" Patrick felt bad about killing the three sea serpents that had survived, but not bad enough to stop David.

"What if the toilet backs up? Then they'll be all over the floor. I have a better idea."

Patrick followed David out of the house. They marched down the block, stopping above the sewer grate on the corner. This was the same sewer they fished tennis and Wiffle balls out of with coat hangers, the balls covered in muck but good enough to play with after a thorough soaking in a bucket of hot water and laundry detergent.

All of the fathers also used the sewer to dump used motor oil, old chemical stuff for their lawns and gardens and basically anything gross and liquid they wanted to get rid of.

It was a fitting resting place for the boys' first bitter disappointment in US commerce.

"You want to say a few words?" David asked with a smirk.

"So long, Amazing Sea Serpents. It was smelly and nasty while it lasted."

David tipped the tank over, the grimy water, sea serpents and sludge balls splashing across the iron grate, pouring through the holes and disappearing into the dark sewer with a soft echo.

"Let's put the tank in Ernie's garbage," David said. "I'm sure that old crank will appreciate the stink."

"Good one."

Ernie was the neighborhood asshole—a man bent on making the lives of every child miserable by chasing them off his sidewalk and even attempting to prevent them from walking in the street by his house.

They snuck to the side of his house and quietly stuck the tank in one of his pristine metal garbage pails. There were several paper bags of trash inside. David hid the tank between two of the bags.

Sprinting away from their dirty deed, they ducked into Patrick's yard, chests heaving.

"No more buying stuff from comics," Patrick said.

"And no more *Wonder Woman*," David added.

Five houses down, in the cloying humidity of the sewer, the remains of the Amazing Sea Serpents seeped into a coagulated mass of muck. There was a faint hiss, then a blue tendril of smoke that twisted down the tunnel.

A wet and ragged rat out for an afternoon of foraging skittered headlong into the smoke. Its body went rigid. It turned and ran as far away from the source of the smoke as it could.

Food could wait.

# Chapter Four

"Time out!"

Patrick waved his arms in the air.

"What for?" his friend Alan said, the bat still in his hand. He was midway between home plate (a chalk outline in the street) and first base (Mr. Arthur's yellow Chevy Nova).

"The ball went down the sewer."

David blurted out, "Ground rule double!"

Alan grumbled. "Man, that would have been a home run. Patrick would have never been able to get it back in time."

"A rule's a rule," David said. He looked back at Patrick, who was four houses away. It was a hell of a blast by Alan, but unfortunately for him, it rolled into the curb and followed the path all the way to ground rule double territory. "You want me to get a coat hanger?"

Patrick stood over the sewer. It smelled worse than usual. But it was a hot summer day.

"I don't know," he replied.

For some reason, he didn't want to get the ball. He kept thinking of the sea serpents and that awful funk. There was no way he was going to touch any ball that came in contact with it.

Instead, he ran to his house. "I have a tube of new tennis balls. I'll go get them."

* * * *

Patrick's alien voice thundered down the sewer.

The black wads of snot from the Amazing Sea Serpent tank were no longer lifeless balls. In the week since their unceremonious dumping into this mélange of waste, they'd sprouted legs and arms and the beginnings of tails. Far from serpents, they resembled a kind of bipedal pollywog.

The pollywogs rolled in the mire, feeding off it, growing more and more each day.

When the ball slipped into the sewer, it crushed one of the pollywogs flat. The thing exploded with a barely audible squish.

The moment the ball rolled away, the other pollywogs descended on their fallen brother, devouring its inky remains with oval mouths filled with tiny points. Food was food.

And lately, they'd been getting very hungry.

\* \* \* \*

It took only a few days for the rats to be fair game for their carnivorous desires. The sea serpents grew exponentially. They needed meat, and there were more than enough rats scampering around the old pipes and pathways.

And scamper they did.

More like ran for their lives.

If anyone would have listened, they would have heard the cries of the rats darting into every tight nook and crevice they could find, desperate to get away from the new alpha beasts in the sewer.

The sea serpents, now the size of cats, weren't necessarily fast, but they worked together. They set traps. While a few scared up a nest of rats, driving them down a long, dark tunnel, the rest waited at the other end, ready to feast.

With each day, each meal, the sea serpents grew bigger, taller, deadlier. Their teeth sharpened, and once-gelatinous stumps at the end of their slimy arms morphed into savage claws.

By the time they cleared the sewer of the entire rat population, they'd evolved into child-sized animals with the appetites of hyenas.

They sensed they must leave the safety of their dank, rotten home. Their instinct for survival fueled their fervent appetite.

When night fell, the sunless sky resembled their dwelling enough for them to skulk from the sewer, the heavy manhole cover an obstacle easily removed.

Martin Henderson's black cat Asphalt peered at the emerging shapes from what it thought was the safety of a row of azalea bushes. It knew these creatures weren't like the other bugs it had chased.

Asphalt didn't detect the sea serpent at its back before it was too late. The black cat's tail was pierced by a razor-like talon, rooting it to its hiding spot. It growled in unmitigated fear.

Little did it know, its cries were nothing more than a dinner bell for the sea serpents.

# Chapter Five

It was over ninety degrees and there was nary a lick of shade outside Shopwell. As much as David and Patrick would have liked to go swimming, they know hot days are the best ones to make money. On days like this, shoppers, especially old people, wanted all the help they could get with their bags.

It was paying off. Their pockets were full to bursting with quarters.

"We could go to the Kendall tomorrow and see that Godzilla double feature," Patrick said, counting out his quarters on the lid of a trashcan. "I've almost got five bucks already."

"And we'll still have plenty left over for the new *Moon Knight* and *Batman*."

Patrick sensed a return of their old debate about which of the two was a better superhero, *Moon Knight* being Marvel Comics' answer to the ever-popular *Batman*, but David looked too tired to fight. They were both sweating up a storm.

"Excuse me, would you boys do me a favor?" An older woman wearing bright red lipstick and so much rouge on her cheeks she looked like a clown stood behind them holding a sheaf of papers in her trembling hands.

David looked around, searching for some bags or a shopping cart.

"I was wondering if you could post these signs for me. I tried, but I'm just not up to it. I'll give you each a dollar."

Patrick said, "Sure, we'd be happy to help."

"Thank you so much. Here, you can use these." She handed Patrick a box of thumbtacks.

David looked at the top flier. It had a picture of a white Yorkie with the word MISSING printed above. The dog's name was Reggie and it had gone missing two days ago. The flier listed a number to call if anyone found Reggie, along with the promise of a reward.

There were tears in the old lady's eyes.

"I miss him so much, but my heart isn't made for this kind of heat."

"I hope someone finds your dog," Patrick said. She patted his head.

"You keep your eyes out, too. You're such nice boys. If I'm going to reward anyone, I hope it's you."

She slowly tottered to her car, which was parked in the yellow loading zone, and drove off, the power steering screeching like a box of angry bats.

David said, "We should put one on the bulletin board inside the store."

"And cool off for a minute."

They walked in the out door. The big corkboard was chock-full of papers. And most of them were notices of missing cats and dogs.

Little Reggie was just one among many. The boys read the pleas to find people's cherished pets until the manager shooed them away.

"I don't mind your little enterprise outside, boys, but I can't have you clogging up the exit."

They left without protest, the heat smacking them in the face.

"What, did someone go around stealing everyone's pets?" Patrick asked.

"I don't know. Come on, let's stick these on some poles."

For thirteen-year-olds, reality is what they make of their own little world. For David and Patrick, that reality revolved around comics, movies, baseball and swimming.

Neither had been aware of the preponderance of missing cat and dog posters popping up all around town the past week. Desperate notices to find lost dogs had been stapled over sad stories of a little girl's cat, Sabrina, that had gone out one day and never returned. It seemed as if there were more missing pets than ones actually safe at home.

"This is crazy," David said.

"Way crazy."

True to their word, and because they wanted to earn that dollar, they found the few bare spots left to put up the missing Reggie fliers. It left them uneasy, at least until they got home and started talking about the Godzilla movies they were going to see the next day.

"You smell that?" Patrick said as they turned the corner to their block.

"Whoever smelt it, dealt it."

"If I beefed like that, call a doctor."

They saw the old jerk Ernie walking away from them, holding a can of something. Thank God he didn't see them. He'd try to tell them he'd bought the sidewalk's rights from the city again and order them off it.

"Maybe Ernie finally cleaned out that garbage can," David said.

Patrick had forgotten that they'd hidden the sea serpent tank in his garbage. He hoped the smell made Ernie sick.

He laughed. "Oh yeah. I bet that made his day."

They high-fived, agreeing to get Alan, Chris, Mike and Jimmy together for a post-dinner Wiffle ball tournament. They also decided to do a little searching for cats and dogs every day. The reward money paid a lot more than hauling bags outside Shopwell or cutting lawns. Everyone's loss would definitely be their gain.

# Chapter Six

"Welcome to Rome! And you know what they say when you're there," Robert Cort said to Bill and Annie Baxter. He held a wooden bowl in his hands. Bill dropped his car keys in the bowl, even though his car was still in the garage around the block.

"You really went all out tonight," Bill said, taking in the decorated yard. Torches lined the rectangular patch of property, casting a warm glow. Roman columns made of cardboard and expertly painted were tacked over the doorway to the house. Bowls of grapes and metal goblets of wine were everywhere. The partiers wore togas, and from what Bill could see when Robert's wife Phyllis bent over to pick something up off the floor, little else. For a woman who'd had three kids, she still had an amazing ass.

"No pressure when it's your turn," Robert said, putting the full bowl down.

"We'll just hire Phyllis to put it together," Annie said. Phyllis ran a local theater, so she had the skills and access to a ton of props.

"You know me," Robert said, offering them some togas. "I don't mind sharing."

Bill and Annie laughed.

These key parties had been Robert's idea two summers ago. Bill thought his neighbor had lost his mind, but when word got around after the first party about what a hit it had been, he'd convinced Annie to at least go to one. She didn't have to do anything she didn't want to do.

That was two years and over a dozen parties ago. He and Annie were old pros by now. Sure, there was still a nervous edge when they walked in, but a little wine and a joint or two helped smooth things out.

"Full house tonight," Bill said. All of the regulars were there, including a new couple. They were younger than most, the wife with radiant red hair and an impressive chest, her hard nipples straining the fabric of the toga. Bill hoped he pulled her key tonight. He'd had everyone else at the party before. It would be nice to try someone new. Annie was eyeballing the husband, too. This could be a very good night, he thought.

And the best part was the sex after the party. He and Annie boinked like teenagers for months after a key party. Each new encounter was a time release aphrodisiac.

"I don't see the Estradas," Annie said.

Robert put on an exaggerated frown. "They called and said they couldn't make it. George has a stomach thing. Next time. Now, get changed and I'll pour some wine."

They walked into the kitchen. There were more bottles of booze on the counter than a proper British tavern. Bill added a bottle of Wild Turkey to the collection. Well-versed with the process, they went to the spare bedroom off the kitchen, stripped down, folded their clothes neatly and placed them next to the other stacks of "regular" clothes.

"Come here."

Bill pressed his body against Annie, his hands gravitating to her ass, their tongues probing. He could feel the heat of her on his growing cock.

"We better save it for later," Annie said, breaking off their embrace with a devilish smile. She slipped into her toga, the hem barely covering the bottom swell of her cheeks.

"And then even later, when we get home."

"And no showering. I want to taste her on you."

Bill's heart fluttered.

He'd heard of endless horror stories about swapping. Real life couldn't be further from the truth. Or at least their real life.

"Hail Caesar!" Bill cried out, swooping his wife into his arms. She giggled, telling him to put her down.

As they exited the spare bedroom, they heard someone cry out.

"They're getting rowdy early," Annie said.

"Or we're just getting a late start," Bill said, stopping in the kitchen to pour a shot of good Scotch and downing it. Mitchell Mc-Grath always brought the high-end stuff. He should. He owned the liquor store on Virginia Avenue.

A man yelled, "What the fuck?"

Bill raised an eyebrow. "I wonder if that's the new guy. He might not understand how things work."

The bottle slipped from his hand when it sounded as if everyone at the party started screaming at once. It landed on top of Annie's bare foot. She cried out in pain, hopping around the kitchen. "Oh, I think you broke my foot."

He didn't have time to console her.

The back door slammed open. Their neighbors tried to cram their way inside. In their excitement, they attempted to get in the house in one big pile. Instead, their bodies wedged in the doorway. It looked like something from a Three Stooges movie.

"What the hell's going on?" Bill said.

He saw Robert's face and his stomach dropped to his balls.

His neighbor was covered in blood. There was a long, ragged gash down the center of his face. His nose was split in half like a bowling alley hotdog.

"Oh my God," Annie screamed, digging her nails into Bill's arm.

As people popped free from the bottleneck, spilling onto the linoleum floor, Bill and Annie could see what was behind the roiling panic.

Black alien bodies reflected the torchlight. To Bill, they looked like oil slicks come to life. Some were feasting on their friends, togas drenched in gore, parts that should be inside now outside. The black beasts, not much taller than a ten-year-old kid, pounced on the back of the people to the rear of the bottleneck. Geysers of blood shot straight into the air.

"We have to get the hell out of here," Bill said.

"I can't walk," Annie moaned, raw terror in her wet eyes.

Bill swept her off her feet, carrying her close to his chest. Someone hit into him from behind, driving him to his knees.

"No, please, no!" he heard Phyllis cry out. It was followed by a sickening squelch of punctured flesh, then the crunch of bone.

The damn things were in the house.

In the bright light, Bill could make them out better—and wished he couldn't.

Bulbous heads that were seemingly all mouth sat atop almost human bodies, with the exception of a thick tail that raked back and forth, knocking people's legs out from under them. As soon as someone went down, another beast was quick to chomp at the softest parts of their exposed flesh.

*The front door!*

He had to get them to the front. All of the creatures appeared to be coming from the backyard.

Everyone else had the same idea, though there were far fewer of his friends and neighbors now. The terrifying black creatures were taking them down one by one.

"Hurry, Bill, hurry!" Annie pleaded. Her arms were locked around his neck so tight, it was hard to breathe.

He got up and sprinted as fast as he could. His heart thumped hard, and he wondered how much longer it could go at this pace before seizing.

A woman, the new wife, scampered past them. Her scalp had been peeled forward, a wet flap of hair hanging over her face. She blindly ran into the dining room table, knocking herself onto her back.

That pause was all the monsters needed to finish her. Her scream was cut off quickly. All Bill heard was desperate gurgling.

Sprinting through the living room, he spied the front door.

"Almost there," he assured Annie.

"They're right behind us!" she shouted in his ear.

Bill got to the door, turned the handle and froze.

It was locked!

"Bill!"

He fumbled for the lock.

Something wet and as hard as cement slammed into his arm, severing it at the elbow. He watched his blood paint the walls and door.

Annie screamed bloody murder. Suddenly, the weight of her was gone. One of the monsters grabbed a thick cord of her hair, yanking her from his grasp.

"Annie!"

There was just enough time to witness the ferocious feast. Everyone was down, flayed open and spilling organs.

He was so engrossed by the carnage, he didn't even feel the mouth clamp onto his face.

* * * *

The key party provided several hours of unadulterated gluttony. The sea serpents ate and ate, grinding bone into a digestible powder, until there was nothing left but shredded togas and pools of coagulating blood.

By the time they were done, they had also grown in height, now well over five and a half feet tall. Their muscles swelled out, limbs thickening.

And they were tired. Satiated.

They fled from the house, silently padding out the door, slinking down the dark street and slipping into the sewer.

Because all of the surrounding neighbors had been at the key party, there was no one left to report the disturbance to the police.

# Chapter Seven

"This sucks if we have to forfeit," Patrick said.

He and David had gotten to the field early. They wanted some extra time to scope the area for any pets. David even brought a collar and leash with him. They had belonged to his dog, Bartie. Bartie, a super cool Labrador that lived to hang around the boys, had been hit by a car last year. He had to be put to sleep. David didn't cry, but he wasn't himself for weeks after.

Unfortunately, Coach Clay arrived early, too. He saw them walking the outfield and made them unload the gear from his trunk. Instead of searching for reward money, they got to take grounders and extra batting practice. Joy.

"We'll lose anyway. The Bobcats are undefeated," David said, eyeing the full team from the next town over.

"Yeah, but I'd rather lose playing than just going home. Where's Alan and Chris?"

David looked around. The parents of the kids on the Bobcats were in full force on their side of the field.

Alan and Chris's parents never missed a game. They were kind of cheesy that way. But they were nowhere to be found today.

"No clue," Patrick said.

The umpire was talking with Coach. Patrick didn't like the body language.

"That's a forfeit," the ump, Mr. Preston, who worked in the hardware store, announced.

"Damn," Patrick said, tossing his mitt to the ground, kicking up a plume of dirt.

"At least now we have more time to look for dogs," David reminded him. "And then there's Godzilla."

Patrick brightened a tad. "I heard they're gonna give out free Godzilla comics in the theater."

"The ones Marvel puts out?"

"No, a special one by the movie studio. Could end up being a big-time collectible."

David punched Patrick's arm. "See, who needs baseball when you have Godzilla and comics?"

"Boys, help me get everything loaded up," Coach Clay called out to the five members of the team that had showed up.

He wasn't happy with the forfeit, either. He'd gone as far as AA ball for the Cleveland Indians and was still insanely competitive. Since the boys who didn't show weren't around to bear the brunt of his tirade, he took his frustrations out on David, Patrick and the other three boys, triplets who manned every outfield position.

"Why the hell do I even bother?" he shouted once all of the parents were gone. The field had cleared out pretty quick, the Bobcats calling them chickens for not playing. "You know how many forfeits I was a part of when I played? And I'm talking from Little League all the way to double A. None. Zero. That's right. It never happened. And you know why? Because we gave a shit. We knew what it meant to be a team."

He threw an olive-colored bag of bats at the backstop. The boys flinched. It looked like every bulging vein in his red neck was going to pop like water balloons. The thought of it almost made David chuckle, but he was smart enough to keep a poker face.

"This is the most humiliating moment of my baseball career."

One of the triplets, a tow-headed kid named Samson, dared to say, "I thought coaching was voluntary, not a career."

Coach Clay turned a venomous glare his way.

"What did you say?"

Samson stammered. "I…I…I'll g-g-get that bag and put it in the trunk." He ran like lightning, lugging the heavy bag into the car and taking off on foot, leaving his brothers behind.

"Tell him he has ten laps waiting for him next practice," Coach Clay told Samson's brothers. They nodded, keeping their eyes on the ground.

After a few more choice words, he told them to get the hell home and show up for an extra night of practice on Monday.

David and Patrick walked home with their bats over their shoulders, gloves hanging off the knobs.

"That was total bullshit," David said. "Why was he ragging on us? At least we showed up."

"He can be a real hammer," Patrick replied. "Maybe we should go to Alan and Chris's house and find out what happened to them."

"Yeah. And then I can chew their butts out like Coach."

\* \* \* \*

Coach Clay stood on the pitcher's mound, staring at the empty outfield, fuming.

*A fucking forfeit!*

He felt bad for taking it out on the boys, but he could have been so much worse. You didn't know what it was like to get your ass handed to you until you screwed up for a minor league coach. Now that was a pro level beat down.

"Hey, Coach!"

It was Samson. He trotted over from the third base side of the field, a ring of keys on his finger.

"I took your car keys by accident."

"Thanks." He wanted to say more, to sound more appreciative, but he was just too wound up.

The smell of garbage—rotted fish and dirty diapers—floated on the breeze. He crinkled his nose.

*Who opened the lid on their filthy garbage cans?*

He turned to look at the row of houses behind home plate. Someone must have had a fish fry two weeks ago and forgot to bring the pail to the curb.

Samson screamed.

When Coach Clay saw the trio of onyx-colored creatures galloping his way, he joined the boy.

He watched in horror as one of the beasts leaped onto Samson. The boy's shouts were cut short as the thing bit his face off as if it were an overripe apple. The coach saw one of the kid's eyes roll out of the mess of gore in the monster's mouth. It hit the dirt, rolling hard and fast until it stopped at his feet. The graying eye looked up at him, as if to say, *Why couldn't you save me?*

There was barely time to look up before he was tackled by the remaining two. He flailed, a wild punch ending with his fist in one of their mouths, bear-trap jaws severing it from his wrist with a horrendous crunch.

The other bit right into his balls. Blood exploded from his punctured groin. Coach Clay tried to scream, but no sound would come out.

Two seconds later, he didn't have a mouth or throat anyway.

# Chapter Eight

While David changed out of his uniform, Patrick went to Alan and Chris's house. Alan answered the door.

"Man, where were you guys?" Patrick nearly shouted. "We had to forfeit the game and Coach Clay went berserk!"

Chris, younger than Alan by less than a year—they were true Irish twins—sidled up next to his brother.

"We couldn't go," Chris said. "We don't know where our parents are."

Patrick laughed. "What, did they run away from home?"

Alan shook his head. His expression was dead serious. "They said they were going to a party last night and they never came back. I called my grandfather and he's coming over. He should be here soon."

The smile dropped from Patrick's face. "That is so weird. I'm sorry."

"My grandfather said they're probably just sleeping it off at whatever house they went to, but I have a weird feeling," Alan said.

"Well, let me know when they come home, okay?"

"Yeah."

The door closed with a soft click.

Alan and Chris were the loudest kids on the block. It was unsettling, seeing them like that.

David called over to him from his porch. "Get your butt changed, bozak! I checked the paper. We can catch the early show if we hurry."

Patrick dipped into his house and got out of his uniform. By the time he met David in the middle of the quiet street, his mind was off his friends and on the king of the monsters.

The Kendall movie theater was only a three-block walk from their house. It was a little on the worn side, but it had a balcony where you could throw candy from and the manager didn't care much if you stayed in there all day.

"What did Alan and Chris say?" David asked, pulling small berries from a bush and tossing them at a parked car, leaving purple splat marks.

Patrick felt guilty for already putting them out of his mind. "They said their parents are missing."

"What?"

"I know. Weird, right?"

"I wouldn't mind if my parents disappeared…at least for a few days. But only after my mom shopped, so I'd have a house full of food."

Patrick recalled the look on his friends' faces. He wasn't so sure getting a break from his parents would be such a cool thing.

The last block to the Kendall was a long, steep hill. Full trees on the corners below obscured the theater.

Virginia Avenue was always busy on a Saturday, but it sounded like there was something really big going on.

"It's too early for the fair," Patrick said. The Virginia Avenue street fair was an annual classic, but that wasn't going to happen until the very end of summer.

"Why is everyone screaming?" David asked.

The boys slowed their pace.

They could hear the commotion loud and clear, but they couldn't make out a damn thing.

There were a lot of shops on Virginia Avenue. Suppose one of them got robbed and there was a whole scene going on with hostages and cops and people running for cover?

Patrick damned his overactive imagination.

But he wasn't imagining those panicked cries.

"Maybe we should just go home," he said.

"Not before we see what the heck is going on," David said, leading the way. Patrick reluctantly followed.

When the Kendall came into view, they stopped, shocked.

Yes, people were running in every direction, screaming their heads off.

But what was causing the riot put the boys' heads in a spin cycle.

"What the hell are those things?" Patrick said breathlessly.

The things trying to grab people outside the Kendall were as black as night, with huge mouths. They had strong legs and thick tails, but their arms were small, like a T. rex's. From here, they looked an awful lot like people in rubber monster suits.

David must have been thinking the same thing, because he started laughing.

"I'll bet that's part of the promotion for the Godzilla movies. They hired some guys to dress up as monsters and scare the balls off everyone. Too cool."

"But wouldn't they just scare people in the theater?" Patrick asked, reluctant to start walking again.

"Nah. This way, the whole neighborhood is focused on the Kendall. Watch. I bet they tell everyone it's all just for fun. Those same monster guys will be handing out the comics when we go inside."

"You're probably right."

"No. I'm *always* right."

They resumed their pilgrimage to the holy Kendall, now the scene of the greatest Godzilla double-feature promotion of all time.

Until they spotted Mrs. Gilchrist, their English teacher, stumble into the middle of the street. Her face smacked right off the asphalt. When she lifted her head up, her nose was smashed flat, blood everywhere.

"Holy cow," Patrick gasped. Now people were getting hurt. She'd end up suing the Kendall and they'd have no more movie theater.

"We should go down there and help her up," David said. No one was paying attention to the older woman. She was on her knees, staring at the blood on her hands.

The boys made it as far as the corner when one of the black creatures grabbed Mrs. Gilchrist from behind, opened its dripping maw and bit her head clean off. When it pulled away, they stared in horror as blood skyrocketed from the stump of her neck.

Patrick grabbed David's shirt, preventing him from taking one step closer.

"What the hell?" David shouted.

This was no promotion.

In their panic, other people were stumbling over one another. As soon as they fell, a creature was there to pounce on them, taking great hunks of flesh as souvenirs.

People were dying!

The beasts were feeding on them!

"We...we have to get out of here," Patrick said, dragging David with him.

"What are those things?"

"I don't know. But we can't stay here."

The creatures had no visible ears. But one of them must have heard Patrick, because it stopped chewing on the back of a man's neck and looked straight at them.

It opened its mouth wide. They saw the rows of pointy teeth, the red, fleshy tongue. Thick, bloody mucous dripped from its narrow bottom lip.

They turned and ran as fast as they could, not daring to look back, not even pausing to vomit, just letting it run freely from their open, gasping mouths as they struggled to get away.

# Chapter Nine

First, they ran to David's house.

"Mom! Dad! Where are you?"

The house was silent.

Struggling to catch his breath, Patrick noticed the note on the kitchen table. He picked it up.

"Hey, your mother took your father to the doctor. Says they'll be home soon."

David's eyes were as white and round as hard-boiled eggs. He looked like he was about to cry.

"They left me?"

"It's not like they knew what's happening on Virginia. Come on, let's go to my house."

When they emerged from David's, they heard the caterwauling of sirens. It sounded like every police car and fire engine was racing toward the carnage outside the Kendall.

*Thank God*, Patrick thought.

Despite terrible stitches in their sides, they sprinted to Patrick's house across the street. His father was home, sitting at the kitchen table eating a ham and cheese sandwich.

"Dad! Where's Mom?" Patrick blurted.

"Out shopping. What's got you two all riled up? You cause whatever all those sirens are running to?" He smiled and took a bite. A talk show about financial investing played on the palm-sized transistor radio that never left his father's side.

Patrick couldn't stop himself from blurting out everything in one long run-on sentence. David just nodded assent next to him.

"Whoa, whoa, whoa, slow down. Did you just say monsters are eating people outside the Kendall?"

"Yes!" they said in unison.

His father shook his head, then took another bite of his sandwich.

"I may be old to you, but I'm not senile. Nice try."

Patrick pulled on his dad's arm, making him drop the sandwich on the floor. His father's right eye twitched. That was always a sign he was getting pissed.

"Thank you for ruining my lunch," he said, swiping his food off the floor and tossing it into the garbage.

David said, "We're not lying and we're not kidding. That's why all the cops are headed down there. These...these things are everywhere and they're attacking everyone."

Even Patrick's father couldn't deny the constant bleating of emergency responders.

"What is going on down there?" he said, walking to the front porch. The sirens were even more ear splitting outside. "You guys stay here. I'm going to check it out."

Patrick jumped in front of him. "Don't go! It's not safe."

Now, there was the crackle of gunfire. Or it could have been firecrackers. Ever since the Fourth of July, kids had been setting off anything left behind a little bit each day.

"You kids stay inside. I'll be right back."

"But Dad, the monsters!"

His father sighed. "Enough about that! I told you, go in the house and wait for me. You got that?"

Patrick saw there was no convincing him or stopping him. His father worked as an emergency medical technician in the city. He was drawn to sirens and bad stuff.

He just had no idea how bad this really was.

"Can you please take your car?" Patrick said.

"Fine. Now do what I said."

They watched him get in the Buick Century and head down the block. Patrick figured once his dad saw the rampaging monsters, he would turn right back and lock the house down.

He was wrong.

They never saw his father again.

\* \* \* \*

"I don't hear any more shooting," David whispered.

The sirens were still going strong. Most of the parents had gone to see what was happening, leaving the kids behind. They stood on porches and front lawns, staring down the street.

No one spoke to one another. There was an air of dread that held their tongues.

Here were all the kids they played ball with, and the little kids they had fun ignoring. It was if they were all strangers to one another.

David couldn't stop looking in the other direction, waiting for his parents' Pacer to come around the corner.

None of the adults were coming back.

"What do we do?" Patrick said so softly David could barely hear him.

"We can't call the police. Who else is there?"

"The army?"

"Doesn't the president have to call in the army?"

"I don't know."

David looked around. "This is freaking me out." He wasn't alone in that department.

"Wait, I think I see someone," Patrick said, pointing.

Sure enough, they spotted a man running, his arms flailing. It looked like he was having a hard time keeping on his feet. The closer he got, the more the boys were able to make out. His face was awash in blood. His shirt was torn down the middle, revealing a jagged line of flayed flesh.

"It's Mr. Gilligan," Patrick said.

Mr. Gilligan was their friend Jimmy's father. He was a bit older than the other fathers, but he was always friendly and never complained about them going in his yard for foul balls or Frisbees.

Now, he looked insane, desperate to flee the terror of what was happening down at the Kendall.

"Help! Help!" he cried.

All of the kids were rooted to their spots. How could a kid help an adult? Especially one that looked to be hurt real bad.

Only Jimmy ran to him. His father saw him and screamed, "Get back, Jimmy! Back in the house!"

"Oh shit!" David gasped. One of those creatures ambled into view. It was following the trail of blood left behind by Mr. Gilligan. It loped, kind of like that hunchback from the Frankenstein movies. But it never slowed its pace. Its mouth kept opening and closing, as if it could already taste Mr. Gilligan.

Jimmy must have seen it too, because he let loose with a high-pitched yelp and turned back toward his house. His father was right behind him.

"Everyone, get inside and lock your doors!" David shouted to the kids. They didn't need to be told twice. The sound of doors slamming filled the air.

He and Patrick were on a high porch. They were the last to heed his own advice.

"What can we do?" Patrick said.

David was about to answer *I don't know*, when the monster lunged forward, tackling Mr. Gilligan. He then fell into Jimmy. With both of them sprawled on the sidewalk, the onyx monstrosity crawled over them, dipped its head and started tearing at their flesh.

Father and son begged for mercy, but there was none to be had.

Patrick clamped his hands over his ears. David knew it was pointless. They'd heard too much already. They would never *not hear* those screams in their heads.

He grabbed Patrick by the elbow. "Come on. We have to lock up."

"Yeah. Windows, too."

While Patrick locked the door, David shut the windows and flipped the latches. It was going to get very hot, very fast.

They lifted the blinds and watched the creature feast on their friend. Jimmy's body shook as it wrested a hunk of meat from his exposed back.

"What is that thing?" Patrick said.

As it ate, it seemed to grow even bigger, the body filling out more, its lashing tail getting thicker, longer.

"You should get your camera," David said.

"Why?"

"So we have proof."

"They're everywhere! Their bodies are the proof."

"I just want to be able to get a closer look," David said. Something gnawed at the back of his brain.

Patrick reluctantly got his Polaroid. It was one of the good ones, with a tele-zoom lens. David quietly opened the window, then the screen. He leaned out as far as he could without falling. Every inch he could get closer was valuable.

His finger found the button for the tele-zoom lens. Suddenly, he could see the monster as clear as day. He snapped off a shot. Waited for the print to stream out, then took another, and another, handing them back to Patrick until the film pack was empty.

When he was done, he shut the window tight.

Patrick had the pictures laid out on the living room table. There were eight grisly shots in all.

As much as it repulsed him to look, David studied every photo, the last couple still developing.

He ran his hand over the stubble on his head and said, "Oh man, I think I know what they are!"

# Chapter Ten

"Is it gone?" David asked.

Patrick stood vigil by the window. He kept the blinds closed, cracking two slats just enough to spy between them.

"Yeah. It took off when there was nothing left of Jimmy or his father."

"Let me see."

Patrick stepped back so David could take a look. He saw that all there was left was a red stain on the ground. Even their clothes had been eaten.

David looked like he was going to be sick. "We have to get to my house."

"I kind of want to be here when my mother comes home."

"Bozak, you know word has gotten out about what happened on Virginia Avenue. The state police probably have all the roads to this area blocked off. If she went shopping at the mall, there's no way they're letting her back here."

Patrick hoped he was right. That was a far better thing to consider than the alternative. He just knew his father wasn't all right. He couldn't have gone down there in the thick of things without getting hurt or worse.

He'd been trying hard not to cry this whole time, but a tear still leaked out from his right eye.

"What's so important that we have to go to your house?" Patrick asked.

"I have to check something. You'll think I'm crazy."

"After what we just saw, nothing's crazy."

"Plus, my house has fewer windows and doors. It's way more secure."

Ever since they had seen *Dawn of the Dead*, they pictured ways to fortify every home, store and building from zombies. These things weren't zombies, but it was even more important to be in as safe a place as possible.

"I'm not going out there without a weapon," Patrick said.

"Your dad have a gun?"

"Not that I know of."

"Then we'll just have to improvise."

David dashed into the basement, advising Patrick to gather all of his baseball bats. They met back in the kitchen.

"Grab everything sharp," David ordered, going for the knife rack. The big carving knife sang when he removed it. Once the floor was filled with knives and cooking forks and baseball bats, David took a roll of duct tape from his waistband. "Let's turn these bats into monster bashers!"

For the next ten minutes, the heavy ripping of duct tape filled the air. The boys taped the utensils, pointed ends facing outward, all along the bats. When they were done, they had four makeshift maces.

"Those things have pretty big heads," Patrick said. "It'll be hard to miss with these."

David swung one of the bats, spearing a loaf of bread on the table. The bag exploded with a loud pop.

"I don't think they'll be so hungry when they get brained. You ready?"

If Patrick could have his way, he'd never leave the house. Armed guards would have to assure him that everything was restored to normal before he stepped foot outside.

But David had always been the leader of their small pack, and Patrick didn't want to look like a wuss. He was also curious to see what was making him risk their lives.

"I'm not locking my door," Patrick said. "Just in case we have to run back in here."

"Smart idea. Okay, on three. One, two, three!"

Patrick opened the door while Dave stepped outside, both bats held before him. If anything had been lying in wait, it would have impaled itself on the knives taped to the end of the bats.

The coast was clear.

The block was eerily silent. There wasn't even a lick of wind.

"Go, go, go," David barked. They ran across the street as if their asses were on fire and the only bucket of water was fifty feet away. They hopped the gate, afraid to undo the metal latch and alert one of those creatures to their presence.

Patrick saw a line of gray muck, like the world's biggest snail trail, snaking past David's house. He prayed that whatever made it was long gone, unlike the cloying stench coming off the trail like waves of heat.

David led the way. They crept along the side of the house, entering the back door that was kept unlocked during the day. Once inside, they dropped the bats, panting.

"See," David said. "That was easy."

Patrick just shook his head, wondering if he was too young to have a stroke. "All right, we're here. Now what?"

"Downstairs."

They clomped down to the still-empty downstairs apartment. David went straight to the garbage can, upending it so the few contents spilled all over the floor.

"It's a good thing I kept forgetting to take out the garbage," he said. "Sometimes putting things off is a good thing."

There was the box they had opened for the Amazing Sea Serpents, along with the empty packets and instruction book. David scooped up the cardboard back with the cartoon of the grinning sea serpent family. He held it close to Patrick's face.

"Look familiar?"

Patrick squinted, studying the comic drawing.

"I don't know what you mean."

"Those creatures outside. Don't you think they look a lot like the Amazing Sea Serpents?"

"Not really, no."

David sighed, exasperated. "Look, they have tails; those things have tails. The sea serpents are standing upright, and so are those monsters."

"But the rest looks nothing like them."

"You remember those weird sludge balls that kept on growing?"

"I'll never forget them, or the stink they made."

"When we were close to them down on Virginia Avenue, didn't the smell seem familiar?"

Patrick sat at the kitchen table, resting his head on his arm. "I was too busy pissing my pants to notice."

David started pacing. "I think those sludge things somehow grew into those monsters. Something in the sewer kept them alive instead of killing them. And now they're too big to stay down there."

Looking up, Patrick said, "I hate to say it, but you might be right. Now that I think of it, they do look a little like those curled-up black balls. At least the head part does."

David flattened the instructions on the table.

"This is all in Chinese or Japanese or whatever. There's no telling what it says."

"Oh yeah, I'm sure it spells out how to turn your dumb pet into a man-eating monster."

David folded the paper and put it into his back pocket.

"We have to find someone who can tell us for sure."

"I'm not going back out there, man."

David rested a reassuring hand on his shoulder. "Look, I don't want to, either. But we may be the only two people who can find a way to stop them."

# Chapter Eleven

David could tell his friend wasn't digging his plan. He might be right. Maybe it was better—and smarter—to just hole up in one of their houses and wait for the good guys to swoop in and clean everything up.

Then he thought of the massacre on Virginia Avenue. The good guys had come, and they were more than likely dead.

Which left him wondering, *What makes me think we'll do any better?*

"Because we know what those things are."

"What'd you say?" Patrick asked. They were poised by the front door, peeking out of the bottom portion of the screen. So far, the street was clear.

"Nothing. Just thinking out loud. Now, the good news is, those things are probably all that way," David said, pointing to their left. "And we're going that way." He pointed to their right. "Totally in the opposite direction."

"There's one word that scares me."

"What's that?"

"*Probably.* It's been over three hours since we saw them outside the Kendall. They could be everywhere by now."

David chewed on a thumbnail, or what was left of it. His old habit had come roaring back, and already most of his nails were down to the quick. "I don't think they're going anywhere for a while yet. There were a lot of people down there. You saw what that thing did to Jimmy and his dad. It didn't even look up until it had eaten every last scrap. There's too much to eat down there. At least for a while."

He tried not to linger on the image of the monster tearing into his friend. Jimmy may have been a know-it-all smartass, but they'd hung around with each other since they were three. He was really going to miss his sarcasm.

David smiled, trying to bolster Patrick's spirits. "Besides, we have these." He hefted one of the weaponized baseball bats.

"I'll do it, but only because I'm faster than you."

David was about to ask what that could possibly mean when it dawned on him.

"Thanks for planning on leaving me to those things, bozak."

"Don't make me have to." Now it was Patrick's turn to smile, pained as it was.

They made sure the door didn't make a sound when they left. Each one watched the other's back as they hopped over the fence onto the sidewalk. David spotted Alan watching them from his living room window. He waved to him with the bat. Alan gave him a thumbs-up. He hoped Alan would decide to come with them, but he had Chris to keep an eye on and Chris couldn't even watch *The Twilight Zone* without having nightmares. There was no way he was leaving the house.

He figured it would take them ten minutes to get to the little strip mall over on Tuckerville Road. That's if they jogged most of the way. Running would be even better, but they had to be careful.

They agreed to stay close to one another, only speaking in whispers.

"Who knows, maybe we'll run right into the police or army," Patrick said.

"You still holding on to the whole army-to-the-rescue thing, aren't you?"

"Isn't that what they do? Save people from danger?"

David wasn't sure where the nearest army base was, but he bet it wasn't anywhere near Tuckerville, which was just outside of Manhattan. Not too much call for military installations in the suburbs.

They kept pace with one another, turning left at the end of Churchill and following Garvin Street for several long blocks. It was beyond weird, not seeing cars on the road or people out and about. They did see plenty of people looking out from their windows, but no one made a move to ask them what they were doing or offer any help.

"This town is full of chickenshits," David said, huffing.

"Maybe someone came by and told them to lock their doors and stay inside."

"Whatever."

David did his best to burn the image of each person and house in his memory. If they survived this, he was going to make sure he never let them live their cowardice down.

They were just about to make the left onto Webley Street when a German shepherd came bounding out of a driveway. It was covered in black slime, with patches of fur missing, bloody flesh exposed. The boys stopped dead in their tracks.

"He looks pissed," Patrick said out of the side of his mouth.

"And hurt. I don't wanna have to kill a dog."

"I don't think he's going to give us a choice."

David choked up on the bat, one of the knives pressing into the meat of his hand.

The dog was barking so loud, so fiercely, foam and spittle flew everywhere. David was sure the whole world could hear.

"Keep it down, boy," he ordered. The dog kept right on growling and barking.

In an instant, its wounded legs sprung. Its mouth was wide open, hungry to tear a chunk of flesh from them. David and Patrick raised their bats but couldn't swing in time.

The German shepherd bowled into them like a missile, the flames of death burning in its cold, black eyes.

# Chapter Twelve

Patrick landed hard on his back. The bat clattered into the gutter. His breath whooshed hot and hurriedly from his lungs.

Straining his head back, he watched upside down as the bloody German shepherd latched onto one of the creatures. It was loping hungrily toward them, downwind, so they hadn't been able to smell it coming, much less hear it.

The oversized sea serpent thrashed and wailed, its cries sounding like a cross between a yowling cat and a trilling blue jay, completely at odds with its massive and deadly appearance. David was already on his feet and trying to lift Patrick up.

"Let's go!" he barked.

Patrick found his bat and ran, glancing over his shoulder at the same moment the sea serpent tore the dog in half.

"Oh crap," he huffed. "It's still coming!"

The sea serpent dragged the halves of the dog, munching on the tail end as it ran. Now, this close, Patrick knew for sure that the things grew as they ate. The creature easily wolfed down the dog the way he'd cram a Pop-Tart into his mouth on mornings when he was late for school. When the thing was done eating, Patrick swore its head was bigger, the legs more muscular, propelling it even faster.

He looked at their bats, realizing with sinking dread that they may as well have been carrying wands for all the good they would do.

They were coming up to the turn onto Tuckerville Road. This was a main thoroughfare for the town. He couldn't remember ever *not* seeing the streets chock-full of cars, even late at night.

Today's traffic report called for empty streets with a commute that could be as quick as you could gun the engine of your car.

Patrick and David ran side by side, but they were slowing down. The day was taking its toll on them, and their legs felt heavy, their ribs aching from taking what seemed like endless streams of deep, worried breaths.

The sea serpent was only ten feet behind them. Patrick could hear and even feel its heavy footfalls through the soles of his sneakers. The wind shifted and the full vileness of its stench hammered them like a billy club.

"Get down, boys!"

The booming voice startled them.

An older man stood on his lawn holding a very imposing rifle. He fired once, the shot buzzing just over their heads. The boys dove to the ground, skinning their knees on the pebbled sidewalk.

Crack! Crack! Crack!

Every shot was a direct hit in the sea serpent's head. The assault stopped it in its tracks. It leaned on its thick tail, arms dangling at its sides, unable to fall completely on its back.

Grayish ichor leaked from the four wounds.

"Great shooting," David said to the man.

He looked at them with wide, glassy eyes, his white hair puffed out like cotton balls on the sides of his head. "I...I did it. You boys should go in my house. The front door's open. You'll be safe."

"We have to get to someplace on Tuckerville Road," Patrick said.

"There's nothing there for you to go to. I have a bomb shelter in my basement. You can stay in there until this blows over."

The monster still hadn't fallen, but it no longer looked like it was breathing. Patrick still couldn't believe that this thing came from a simple, stupid Amazing Sea Serpents kit.

"That's okay," David said, grabbing Patrick by the elbow. "Thank you for saving us. We'll be fine."

The man glared at them with narrowed eyes, his lips drawn tight. "I'm not asking you, boy. I'm telling you. It's for your own good."

"No, really, we can take it from here," David replied, sounding very nervous.

Patrick was transfixed by something else.

He watched the bullet holes start to close up, the puckered flesh flattening out, stopping the rush of vital fluids from pouring forth. The sea serpent's chest heaved once...twice.

"Uh, David."

"Now get inside before I get angry."

Patrick's stomach dropped when he saw the rifle pointed at him. The old man looked mad enough to spit nails.

David whispered out the side of his mouth, "We can't go in there. That's the pervert everyone talks about. They say he went to jail for messing with a ten-year-old boy."

Patrick looked past the man at the worn colonial house behind him, suddenly realizing it was the place parents warned them never to go near. Patrick's father made him promise he would always cross the street when he came near it and never, ever engage the man who lived there.

The hammer clicked back on the rifle.

"I'll give you boys to the count of two."

Patrick jumped when the revived sea serpent used its tail to launch itself at the aging pederast, sailing the fifteen feet between them with savage ease. It soared onto him from above like a bird swooping down for a fat worm. It opened its mouth wide, swallowing the man from the head all the way to the middle of his chest.

The rifle went off. David spun on his heels, crying out.

The sea serpent gnawed on the man as if he were a hunk of rawhide.

"Are you hit?" Patrick asked, wondering what the hell he would do if David was shot and couldn't keep going.

David had a hand over his upper arm. A small trickle of blood snaked down to his elbow. He pulled his hand away. There was a bloody furrow in his flesh.

"I think it just grazed me, but it burns like hell."

"Can you run?"

"Of course I can. He shot my arm, not my legs."

"Well then, hurry up, before he finishes eating the kid toucher."

The old man was much more substantial than the dog. The sea serpents couldn't seem to break away from a meal once they started. Hopefully that would give the boys enough time to get well away from this one.

Patrick and David dashed onto Tuckerville Road. The shops were empty, the entire street closed up, probably for the first time ever.

"We're screwed," David said.

They kept running, wanting to put as much distance as they could between themselves and the masticating sea serpent.

Then Patrick saw something in the distance, right where the funeral home would be.

"Maybe not yet," he said, using the little stores of energy he had left to pick up the pace.

# Chapter Thirteen

The police had the entire southern end of Tuckerville Avenue cordoned off. David and Patrick ran toward the flashing lights and sawhorses. Along with the cops were dozens of regular people who looked to have been out enjoying their day before hell spilled all over Tuckerville. The small crowd breathlessly watched their approach.

There didn't look to be anyone in an army uniform. David wasn't surprised, but he couldn't help feeling disappointed.

He dared to take a quick peek behind them and saw there were no ravenous sea serpents.

A pair of cops pulled a sawhorse aside, letting them through.

"You boys okay?" one of them asked. He had a thick brown mustache with bits of crumbs in it.

Now that they could really stop and catch their breath, both boys bent over at the waist, hands on their knees, struggling to regulate their breathing.

David felt a strong hand on his shoulder. "Just take a moment, son."

He heard a woman say, "I can only imagine what they went through."

Patrick started dry heaving, a long line of spittle hanging from his lower lip.

"One…of them…was chasing…us," David said between ragged breaths. "But I think…we lost…it."

"Where did you last see it?" the mustached cop asked.

David pointed. "About four blocks."

The cop spoke into his walkie-talkie. "Just got confirmation that they're spreading out. Send the wagon here with everything you've got."

"You all right, Pat?" David asked.

His friend wiped his mouth clean with the back of his hand. "I'll never complain about gym class again. I'd rather have Mrs. Kazeroski screaming at me to do four laps than run like that."

The cop asked them, "Was it just one creature, or were there more?"

"Just one," Patrick answered.

The cop looked to his partner, concern etched on his face, mustache twitching. "Well, there goes the theory that they hunt in packs. I supposed that would have made things too easy."

"Bullets can't kill them," Patrick said.

Now a ring of cops surrounded them. "Come again?"

"I watched it. The one that was chasing us got shot four times in the head. The bullets stopped it for a while, but then the wounds healed up in like a minute and it ate the man who shot it."

A heavyset cop with beads of sweat running down his flabby cheeks huffed. "I'm sure that's what you think you saw."

David looked at him as if he were three sandwiches short of a full picnic basket. "Oh, so all the other stuff that's happened today makes total sense?"

A couple of the cops snorted with controlled laughter. The fat cop peeled away from the circle, muttering under his breath.

The mustache cop said, "Tell me exactly what you saw."

After they were done, they were told to walk to the diner behind the cordon so someone could get them to a safer place. In fact, the police announced that everyone had to clear the hell out, pronto.

In the bit of chaos that ensued, Patrick and David slipped away from the crowd hustling to the idling police vans.

David said, "Man, I hope he's still there."

Patrick dipped between the chrome fenders of two parked cars, angling after David. "I still don't know where we're going."

"To the hibachi place."

"You almost got us killed so we could get teriyaki steak?" He looked like he was about to punch David square in the mouth.

"No, you bozak." He pulled the instructions from his back pocket. "We're going to find Carl. I bet he can read this."

Carl was their favorite hibachi chef. In fact, whenever their families went to the restaurant, they requested Carl, opting to wait if they had to. Carl was not only a true hibachi showman; he was also extremely funny, never forgetting a face or a name. He greeted them like they were family returning from a long trip.

And he was the only Asian person they knew in Tuckerville.

"They're coming!"

David and Patrick froze. A trio of sea serpents, now a staggering ten feet tall, had burst out of a manhole right next to the police barricade. The lead sea serpent reduced a sawhorse to splinters with a swipe of its hand, tearing the face off the cop with the mustache.

Everyone started shooting. The noise was deafening.

Bodies flipped into the air. Men and women screamed.

And the blood!

In seconds, it was everywhere. In the air, spilling onto the ground, staining the faces of those trying to kill the creatures as well as those desperately seeking safety.

One of the sea serpents took on so much lead, David was sure it would be ripped into pieces. The shotgun shells and bullets merely slowed it down, but not enough to stop if from tearing into people as if they were paper dolls.

These monsters were so big, they seemed unstoppable.

"We gotta go," David said, staring at the melee. "Before they see us."

Patrick didn't need to be told twice. They ran behind the diner, sticking to the back lots as they made their way to the hibachi restaurant.

The shriek of the sea serpents and death cries of their victims followed their every step.

# Chapter Fourteen

The smell of rotting fish signaled their arrival.

Out back with all the dumpsters, it was hard to tell where they were. The hibachi restaurant sold this raw fish nastiness called sushi. The sun blazing down on the dark blue dumpsters made it easy for a blind person to find it.

They scooted to the front just to make sure.

Patrick looked like was going to start bawling.

"It's closed."

"I figured it would be. We have to go upstairs."

The restaurant occupied the bottom floor of a two-story building. David had heard his father say that some of the workers lived in the apartments on the second floor. He hoped his father was as right about that as he was about not wasting money on phony crap in comic book ads.

They started to climb an exterior flight of stairs, the two boys too worn out to go any faster than a brisk walk. The white paint was flaking off the risers and banister like psoriasis scabs. Paint chips flecked the palms of their hands.

Since there was no doorbell, the boys pounded on the door. They heard people talking in Japanese, but no one was answering.

"We're not monsters," Patrick said.

The door suddenly swung open. One of the busboys stood in the doorway, looking like he was going to crap himself blue.

"Is Carl here?" David said.

"Yes," the busboy replied with a heavy accent. "I'll get him."

He shut the door on them, even going so far as to lock it. David and Patrick stood on the small platform, breathing through their mouths to avoid the dumpster smell…or could it be the sea serpents getting closer? If those things spotted them up here, they were dead meat.

No one was shouting anymore. All was silent, which meant those sea serpents were feeding.

They heard the door unlock and Carl was there, clearly annoyed. "I'm sorry he was too ignorant to let you in. Please, come inside."

The apartment was spotless. Several men they recognized from the restaurant got up from the living room couch and filed down a long hallway.

"Privacy," Carl explained. He poured them each a glass of water from the tap. David and Patrick greedily sucked the water down, not realizing until this moment how parched they'd been.

"You boys should not be outside," Carl said. "The police have ordered everyone to stay in their homes. Do your parents know where you are?"

David thought about his parents, wondered where they could be, hoped they were safe. Patrick's shoulders sagged.

"Carl, do you know why the police have everyone on lockdown?" David asked.

Carl shook his head. "It must be very serious."

"You have no idea how serious."

"Still, David, where are your parents? I hope you did not sneak out of your house because you were curious. That kind of curiosity can get you killed."

"Like the cat," Patrick said, his voice far off.

"There are these huge, black monsters running around eating everything in sight," David said. "They've come up from the sewer. We saw them slaughter a bunch of people on Virginia Avenue, and now they're headed this way."

Carl studied both of them, looking for a trace of a lie.

"Didn't you hear all the people screaming, and the gunshots?"

"Yes. We all thought it was some kind of attack. Maybe a robbery gone bad."

David handed over the Amazing Sea Serpents instruction page. "Do you have any paper and a pencil?"

"Yes. Why?"

"Patrick is a great artist. He can draw what's out there."

Carl went to the kitchen and got a pencil from a drawer, along with a brown paper bag. He gave them to Patrick.

Patrick didn't just love to read comics; he was also an expert at drawing all of the superheroes. His life goal was to draw for Marvel Comics one day. David didn't doubt he'd do just that. His Thing looked better than the way the professional artists drew him in *The Fantastic Four*. His detail work was amazing, and he worked fast.

While Patrick drew the sea serpents, David explained.

"You see, we ordered these Amazing Sea Serpents from a comic book. They were supposed to be these little fish things, I guess, but they turned out to be just blobs. The kit came with this."

Carl started reading the paper, his brows knit close together.

"When nothing grew like it should have, we kind of dumped them in the sewer."

Carl's hand flew to his mouth, his lips moving but no sound coming out.

"Where did you get this?" he asked.

"I told you. We ordered it from a comic book."

"This did not come *from* a comic book."

"Well, it came from wherever they make these things, but we ordered it from a comic book."

Carl paced the room, reading the paper again.

"Here," Patrick said, holding out the paper bag.

He'd rendered a perfect likeness of the sea serpents, right down to their oversized mouths and claw-tipped fingers. Carl took one look and thumped his back against the wall. He slowly slid down until he was sitting, staring at the sea serpent instructions and Patrick's drawing.

"This is an abomination," he said, more to himself than the boys.

"It's worse than that," David said.

"You do not understand. What you hatched were Hakuri, the Demon Lizards of Hatsukaichi. These are not children's pets. They are devourers of worlds."

# Chapter Fifteen

"Demon lizards?" Patrick said. "I thought they were supposed to be fish or something."

"These are not the things from your little comic books!" Carl yelled. The boys flinched. They'd never seen Carl without a smile, much less flipped out and screaming.

He rubbed his eyes and exhaled. "I am so sorry. I should not have shouted at you. The instructions call them Amazing Hakuri, not sea serpents. When I saw your drawing, it frightened me."

"It's okay," David said. "We've had worse happen to us today. So, you really know what these things are?"

Carl got back on his feet. "I know in the sense that I am aware of a terrible legend handed down where I grew up. I am sure you have both heard of Hiroshima."

David and Patrick nodded.

"Were you there when the atom bomb fell?" Patrick asked.

The faint flicker of a smile played on Carl's lips. "No, Patrick, I was not born yet. Hiroshima is very close to Hatsukaichi. It is said that the Hakuri were first spawned in Hatsukaichi in the fifteenth century. One day, after a terrible storm, there followed an earthquake. The ground split in two. Many strange things rose up from the great fissure. The Hakuri eggs scattered into the air, spawning in pools and lakes. They quickly grew into killing and eating machines. They descended on the countryside like locusts, consuming everything in their path. Thanks to some very wise men, they were stopped. But they have returned once every century since, always in a different prefecture. It appears someone has taken it upon themselves to make sure their return did not happen in my home country; someone without a conscience, as evil as the Hakuri. In Japan, it is important to stop them before they grow to an unmanageable size. Tell me, how big are the ones you saw?"

"The tallest had to be ten feet. They're probably even bigger now that they've been eating all those cops," Patrick said.

Carl paled.

"That is not good."

David seized on the one ray of hope. "You said that in Japan, you know how to stop them."

"Yes, but only when they are much smaller. They have one weakness, but they may have gotten too strong for it to work."

"Kryptonite can stop Superman," Patrick said. "If he can be beaten by a tiny rock, there's gotta be something that can stop these Hakuri."

Someone outside screamed. They ran to the front of the apartment. The other men—chefs, waiters, busboys,—crowded around the windows.

One of the sea serpents—the Hakuri—was across the street. It had a woman in a bear hug, her head in its mouth. It was so big, it could reduce the building to rubble if it decided to charge it like a bull with its massive head lowered.

A man from the apartment came out and shot the Hakuri with a handgun. The Hakuri whipped its tail, sending the man flying through a plate-glass window. It did this without pausing its flailing repast.

All of the men turned to look at Carl and the boys. Their mouths quivered in fear.

"Weapons will not be enough," Carl said. "There is only one thing that may work. And luckily, we have much of it. We just need to go downstairs to get it."

The men began shouting in Japanese. Carl tried to restore order, but David didn't have to know the language to understand that they were freaking out.

Carl snapped at them and they quieted.

"I will go to the restaurant. I have the key to the back door. You boys remain here where it is safe."

"Nowhere's safe," Patrick said.

"Then *safer*," Carl said.

David trailed after him. "What kind of weapon can a hibachi restaurant have? Is it the raw fish?"

Carl slipped on a pair of running shoes.

"No. It is wasabi. It is like acid to the Hakuri. Now, stay put!"

He stepped out onto the landing, locking the door behind him.

David and Patrick looked to one another and said simultaneously, "Wasabi?"

\* \* \* \*

The moment he stepped out the door, Carl felt as vulnerable as a newly hatched chick. His high vantage point gave him a good view of the back end of the strip of stores, restaurants and the First Federal Bank.

All was clear.

But that could change in the blink of an eye.

He wasted no time, clambering down the steps as quickly and quietly as he could, the rotted wood cracking loud as fireworks, or at least that's how it seemed to him.

The key slipped easily into the lock. He entered the kitchen, locking the door behind him. The basement door was to his right.

Carl flicked on the light and descended. What he needed was stacked on a small pallet in the back.

He counted six boxes in total. He hoped it would be enough.

Each box was filled with wasabi stems, grown along riverbanks in various farms around Japan. The pungent, hot condiment had been gaining popularity in their restaurant, now that more and more people were coming in for the sushi. The hibachi side of the restaurant was still the moneymaker, but he'd been pleased to see their patrons willing to explore something so exotic, at least for their taste.

Every morning, the staff opened a box of wasabi stems, finely grating it as they did fresh ginger root.

He was able to carry two of the boxes back up to the kitchen. Once there, he grabbed half a dozen oroshigane graters. They would be very, very busy for the next hour, preparing the only thing that could stop the Hakuri, if they could even be stopped now.

*Amazing Sea Serpents!*

These Hakuri were much like the ones he'd heard about growing up, but something was different. They were altered somehow, their growth accelerated. America was a much different land than Japan. The Hakuri were highly adaptable. Whatever toxins resided here would only serve to fuel their abnormal growth.

What evil mind infiltrated a toy company, willing to sell such horrid creatures to unsuspecting children? Perhaps they were simply misguided, only wanting to spare Japan. Still…

And where did they find their eggs?

So many questions, but no one to answer them.

For now, the only thing to worry about was killing the Hakuri.

As Carl turned the lock to exit the back door, he heard the front plate-glass window shatter. The floor thundered with the reverberations of immense footfalls.

Carl slipped out the door, making sure to lock it behind him.

He ran to the apartment, the top box teetering, wondering if the boys had been minutes too late in coming to him.

# Chapter Sixteen

"We saw it go in the restaurant!" Patrick exclaimed the moment Carl burst through the door.

"We do not have much time. Quick!"

He handed out what looked like handheld cheese graters to everyone, tearing the lids off the boxes. One of the busboys—Patrick wished he knew his name—dashed to the kitchen and got bowls for everyone.

Carl gave them each handfuls of what looked like thick, green tree roots.

"We must grate as much as we can. Boys, grate the wasabi over the bowl and be careful. The oroshigane is extremely sharp."

David got right to work. "I help my mom in the kitchen all the time. After everything, I'm not worried about cutting my finger."

Carl's frantic gaze bore into both of them like hot pokers. "You must not get blood in the wasabi. It will make it powerless."

Patrick took a deep breath, grabbed a root and started grating, slowly at first. "Okay, no blood in the wasabi."

While they worked, the building shook as the sea serpent went hog wild in the restaurant.

The other men worked in total silence, sweat streaming down their faces.

"Why is that sea serpent down there?" Patrick asked, picking up the pace.

"The Hakuri have a very good sense of smell," Carl said, his arms working so fast, his hand was a blur. "It knows the method of its destruction is here. It wants to obliterate it."

David smirked. "Yeah, well, they have a very distinctive smell of their own."

The reek of spoiled fish and hot garbage made its way through the floorboards.

A sudden thought made Patrick stop grating the wasabi. "Wait, that means it can smell what we're doing up here?"

Carl didn't raise his head from his task. "Yes. So grate faster!"

The bowls were filling with the acrid paste, used up roots tossed to the floor. It sounded like the sea serpent had gotten into the kitchen and was ripping appliances from the floor, tossing them around like toy blocks. No one could stop themselves from flinching with each crash.

"What do we do with all this wasabi once we grate it?" David asked, his tongue poking out of the side of his mouth while he worked.

"I will figure that out when the time comes," Carl replied. "Now, no more talking."

Patrick's stomach flipped like a flapjack when he heard the distinctive sound of the back door exploding, metal screeching on the concrete.

One of the men got up and looked out the small window facing the yard. He said something in Japanese. Carl stood up and went to the kitchen. Out of a drawer he took a knife that looked as if it could fillet a whale.

Using a paper towel, he coated both sides of the long blade with wasabi.

With one hand on the doorknob, he looked to Patrick and David. "You did a very good thing, coming to me. No matter what happens, all of you take the wasabi and find someone in authority. Tell them they must dip all of their weapons in wasabi. Fill buckets of it if they can. With luck, the Hakuri will slumber for another hundred years."

"Carl, don't!" Patrick pleaded, but it was too late. Their favorite hibachi chef was out the door, blade held high.

Everyone ran to the window.

With a loud war cry, Carl rushed down the stairs.

The sea serpent looked up at him with its tiny, obsidian eyes. It was easily twice his height and four times wider. Patrick remembered the story of David and Goliath from CCD class. He'd always thought it was just a fairy tale. If Carl somehow defeated the sea serpent, he'd never doubt it or anything else Sister Marie taught him again.

Midway down the creaking stairs, Carl leaped over the banister, hurtling toward the sea serpent from above.

The sea serpent spread its stunted arms as if to hug a long-lost friend. Its hideous mouth opened wide.

The blade sliced right down its throat, along with most of Carl's arms. The sea serpent caught him, immediately locking its arms around his waist and squeezing.

Carl's scream nearly made Patrick wet his pants again.

"Holy crap!" David said, glued to the horrific spectacle.

Carl drove the knife deeper, cutting off the sea serpent's wails. The veins on the sides of Carl's neck bulged until they began to burst, mini volcanoes rupturing on a smooth coastline of flesh.

Great gouts of green foam spilled from the sea serpent's mouth.

"Look!" Patrick said, pointing at its flat belly.

The foam burned its way through the creature's stomach, splattering onto its feet. The sea serpent's tail swished violently back and forth, its knees buckling. Carl rolled free, his face blue, body as lifeless as a rag doll.

The sea serpent melted from the inside out, retching up half-digested human remains, blood and more of that welcome, verdant froth.

It took several minutes for it to die, but die it did, collapsing onto itself like a deflating jumping castle.

"Poor Carl," Patrick said, his hand on the window. He could feel everyone's hot breath on the back of his neck.

David broke their mourning for Carl. "We need to make a whole lot more wasabi."

Heads nodded and they went back to work.

Within the hour, they had enough wasabi to do some serious damage.

"We need to get this to the right people," Patrick said.

They stared at the door, knowing they had to leave the relative safety of the apartment. But at least they now had a chance to survive.

"Unless *we're* the right people," David said.

The boys carried ten sealed bowls of fresh wasabi. The moment they stepped outside the door, it slammed behind them, the lock snapping with sharp finality.

"Chickenshits," David shouted at the door. More people to add to his list.

Patrick looked at the bowls in his arms. "At least they made the wasabi."

# Chapter Seventeen

Tuckerville Road was as quiet as a cemetery at night, and filled with just as many bodies.

Well, the scattered remains of as many bodies.

The sea serpents had done a pretty thorough job of digesting as much of every victim as they could, but there were still stray limbs, a few fingers, the top of a scalp, odd bits of clothes and shoes and, draped over a parking meter, the flap of someone's entire face.

"Oh man, that's gross," Patrick said.

Their eyes darted in every direction as they walked down the middle of the street, waiting for a sea serpent to attack.

They'd hoped to find someone alive, maybe even a cop who'd survived the massacre who could radio in what they knew.

Luck was not their lady today.

"Okay," David said. "I say we get back home, where it all started. If the phones are still working, we can call the cops and tell them, not that they'll believe us. Then I think we need to dump some of this wasabi in the sewer."

"Why the heck would we waste it?"

"Maybe they have a nest down there, with little ones still growing. We need to destroy everything."

"We? We're just kids."

"Yeah, kids who know what those things are and how to kill them. Kids who will also be told to be quiet and let the grown-ups do the work. While we wait, more people will die."

*Maybe even my parents*, David thought, *if they're not dead already.*

Just then, a sea serpent came tearing around the corner of Tuckerville and Grassy Sprain road. It must have spotted them first, anxious for its next meal.

David ripped the top off of one of the containers. The waves of wasabi stink stung his eyes.

Patrick did the same.

They put the other containers down, holding their ground, waiting. The sea serpent wasn't as big as the one Carl had fought, but it could still probably eat them in one bite.

"Holy crap, I'm scared," Patrick said, his legs shaking.

"Me too, bozak. Just make sure you don't miss."

The sea serpent got overanxious, using its tail to take to the air to cover the last few feet. The boys stepped away from one another, chucking the wasabi at the creature as it sailed between them. The wasabi peppered its flesh with a hot hiss. Green scum bubbled on its slick skin.

When it hit the ground, it stayed there, writhing in agony. The wasabi ate away at it the way the creature ate people, with unrelenting efficiency. David's muscles remained coiled, ready to dump more wasabi if he needed to.

He didn't.

He and Patrick bashed it with their bats, the blades slicing deep, rending great, seeping gashes in its flesh.

The sea serpent let out a final breath that smelled like Satan's fart. The boys backed away, fanning the air.

"Well, that worked," David said, unable to keep the quaver from his voice. They'd killed it, but he'd almost had a heart attack in the process.

Patrick's face lit up. "Yeah, we did. Holy cow, we did. Let's go home!"

Strengthened by confidence, they ran, slower now that they were carrying all the wasabi and their legs and lungs were worn out.

\* \* \* \*

They were two blocks from their houses when another sea serpent, this one only about their size, popped out of a sewer like a slice of bread from a toaster. It scared Patrick right off his feet, some wasabi spilling on his shirt. David hoped it would keep the monster from biting his friend.

"Take a long walk off a short pier," David said, tossing a handful of wasabi in the sea serpent's face. The acid sizzled and the beast flipped backward, falling into the open sewer. Its death cries echoed in the deep, dark tunnel.

"It should have put the manhole cover back," Patrick joked. David grabbed his hand, lifting him to his feet.

David's house was on the left, Patrick's on the right. David said, "Get your BB gun and meet me at my house. I have an idea."

When Patrick left, David went to Alan and Chris's house. The boys were reluctant to answer, but looked relieved when they saw it was him through the window.

"Why are you carrying a bunch of Tupperware?" Alan asked.

"The stuff in here kills those things," David replied, breathlessly. "You want to help us kick their asses?"

Chris snorted. "I seriously doubt leftovers will kill them."

"This ain't leftovers. It's fresh made and deadly. Trust me. Pat and I just killed two of them getting back here. You still have your bow and arrows?"

The brothers took archery lessons and were pretty good shots.

"Of course we do," Alan said.

"Get them and come to my house. Hurry!"

David was deflated to walk in his door and find his parents still hadn't returned. He shook all negative thoughts away. He had a job to do.

Patrick was the first to arrive. He'd put the bowls and his BB gun and a box of BBs in a lawn bag. He emptied the contents out on David's living room rug. Alan and Chris showed up next. They had four quivers loaded with arrows.

"And here's my contribution," David said, emptying his box of contraband Chinese throwing stars. He'd been buying them on the sly from the headshop down on Virginia Avenue. His parents had banned them from the house after he got busted in school launching them at a telephone pole. How was he to know Karen Fitzgerald was going to walk past the one time he didn't hit his mark?

He was exceedingly glad he'd kept buying them, storing them under his bed.

"All right, now what?" Alan asked.

"Make sure you get this stuff all over everything," David said, opening the wasabi.

The brothers cringed. "Smells nasty," Chris said.

"It burns them like acid," Patrick said. "Stops them right in their tracks."

While they worked getting wasabi on the arrowheads, throwing stars and BBs, David and Patrick told them everything Carl had revealed. The brothers took them at their word, anxious to see how the wasabi worked.

Patrick said, "Carl told us that they have a very good sense of smell. One of them came right for the restaurant because it got the wasabi's scent. I say we just go outside and let them come to us."

David was impressed by Patrick's newfound bravery. Maybe they really were superheroes now.

All four boys carried the wasabi and weapons outside, standing in the middle of the street, facing north, south, east and west. They opened all of the Tupperware bowls, letting the wasabi scent waft on the summer breeze.

They waited, taut as guitar strings.

"Maybe we should have seen you guys kill one of them before we agreed to this," Chris said, an arrow notched in the bow.

He was answered by a multitude of high-pitched cries.

David had a throwing star in each hand.

"Here they come!"

# Chapter Eighteen

And come they did.

Sea serpents cantered down both ends of the street. There had to be at least forty of them, all in different sizes, which meant some were eating better than others.

"I need to take a shit," Alan said.

"Join the club," David said.

"Chris, are they close enough for you guys?" Patrick asked.

Chris sighted down the arrow. "Yep."

"Let 'er rip!"

The arrow flew straight and true into the lead sea serpent. It hit with a wet *thunk* right between its eyes. Green spume exploded from the wound. The creature fell face-forward, twitching madly while the others trampled over its body.

"Holy shit, it worked," Alan said. He followed with a direct hit of his own. Chris let another one sail.

The sea serpents kept coming, but their numbers were thinning.

"My turn," Patrick said. He estimated there was just enough distance between them now for his BBs to hit home. He pulled the trigger rapidly, moving from one creature to the next. Little blasts from the $CO_2$ cartridge spewed the BBs in an arcing line.

He knew they hit from the gouts of green erupting from the sea serpents' flesh, but the BBs were too small, delivering too tiny a payload to drop the beasts with the cold efficiency of the arrows.

"Oh damn," he said.

David sidled up next to him and threw a star as hard as he could, grunting. The star caught one in the leg and it collapsed, screeching as it pawed at its melting appendage.

"Looks like we need to team up," he said.

"Like Green Arrow and Green Lantern," Patrick said.

David gestured toward the brothers. "They're Green Arrow. We're like Power Man and Iron Fist!"

The boys let loose with everything they had. The sea serpents' attack started to slow as the lumbering monsters got tangled up in the writhing mass of the dying. As soon as they hit the ground, an arrow, BB or star, each wasabi dipped, found its way into their backs, finishing them off.

But some were still getting close. Too close.

"The bowls!" David shouted. He and Patrick grabbed several bowls, running toward the charging sea serpents. They emptied the contents on them, the spray pelting multiple creatures at once. Their ghastly flesh popped and fizzled, small holes expanding to gaping chasms, the inner stuff that was muscle and sinew pouring out like hot lead.

The sea serpents howled. One of them kept charging blindly, the wasabi melting its eyes and collapsing its head. It knocked into Alan, whose shot went wild.

"Get it off me!" Alan screamed.

David poured more wasabi on it, enough to get it to scramble away and off his friend.

"Give me a bowl," Chris demanded.

The remaining sea serpents were too close for arrow work. It was going to be wasabi-to-claw combat from here on in.

The four boys tossed wasabi like they would douse each other with the hose on a hot day. The stench of frying sea serpent flesh and muscle was so bad, it made their eyes water.

But they fought through the blurry haze.

Claws and tails lashed out, slicing the boys on the arms and legs. One just missed disemboweling David, who was quick enough to jump back, only receiving a burning slash on his midsection.

Another lodged a claw in Patrick's hand. Patrick grunted, the agony making his head spin. Just like Captain America would explain his acrobatics in the comics, Patrick went with the momentum of the monster's downward swipe. By doing that, he was able to pull the top of his hand out from the claw. The sea serpent teetered, off balance. Patrick finished it off by dumping wasabi on the back of its skull while it hit the ground.

The fallen sea serpents, covered in wasabi, acted as a kind of barrier around the boys, the poison consuming them enough to take down the others. One step in the acidic miasma was enough to begin the process of putrefaction. For beasts so terrifyingly deadly, it didn't take much to melt them like the Wicked Witch of the West.

When the gang was done, they were surrounded by dead and dying sea serpents. Some of the bodies had melted entirely, black goo running down the gutter into the sewer.

Patrick followed the path of the liquid remains.

"We've got one more thing to do."

# Chapter Nineteen

David was the first to step off the iron ladder and into the sewer. It was as hot as hell and smelled, the humidity hovering around a thousand percent.

Patrick, Alan and Chris followed.

There weren't many arrows left, and Patrick was close to running out of BBs.

"We just need to check for a nest," David said.

"More like a spawning ground," Patrick said. "I don't think these things make nests like birds."

"I don't mean a literal nest."

"It would have been smart if one of us brought a flashlight," Chris said.

Patrick looked at David, who just shrugged. They'd already done more than any of the police or other adults. They couldn't be expected to prepare for everything.

"Hopefully we don't have to go far. When we dumped them, they had to land right about here."

There was nothing but sludge and trickling water by their feet. No sign of sea serpents or their eggs.

"That's good, because there's no way I'm going down those tunnels," Alan said. He had a nasty bruise on his leg where the sea serpent had barreled into him.

"Well, maybe all we need to do is follow our noses," David said. "They're pretty hard to miss."

Chris pinched his nostrils. "It smells like the inside of a sweaty ass crack down here. How will we be able to tell? It can't get any worse."

They scanned the sewer floor, shifting the muck around with the tips of their Pro Keds.

David ventured the farthest. Water dripped from somewhere in the distance, the sound bouncing off the walls.

Alan kept an arrow notched in his bow.

"Just don't accidentally hit us," Patrick said.

David stepped on something that gave way with a foul squish. He looked down. His sneaker was covered in a black mound of what looked like watery elephant dung. White maggots crawled out of the mess, slithering onto his bare leg.

Worst of all, they were making tiny squealing noises. It made his balls retreat to the back of his throat.

He jerked away, slipping on the wet surface and falling in the water. Some of it got in his mouth. His stomach sent it right back with the intensity of having consumed a bottle of ipecac.

"You okay?" Patrick said.

David looked at the gross nightmare of mud.

There were little black eggs within it. One of them rolled onto his hand. It looked exactly like the sludge balls in the Amazing Sea Serpents tank.

"I found it!" he said, spitting the dregs of vomit out. "There's a whole bunch of them. Bring the wasabi."

Patrick came over with an open container. He cringed when he saw the disgusting pile of eggs and filth.

"Bombs away," he said, spilling the wasabi all over it. The eggs popped like little firecrackers, releasing intense bursts of noxious gas. Their diminutive death shrieks bounced off the filthy sewer walls. David, his face so close to it, threw up again.

Some of the sludge balls tried to roll free, but David was too quick, squashing them under his sneakers. They exploded in tiny bursts of black and red. It felt real good.

The other boys joined him, stomping any of the retreating sea serpent larvae. When they were done, they were covered in sweat, panting, sucking in the vile, tainted air.

"Did we get them all?" Alan asked.

"Yeah," David said, regaining his footing. He leaned against the tunnel wall, felt slime at his back and jerked away. "Let's get the hell out of here."

Chris said, "I don't think I'll ever be able to eat again. My stomach feels like it died."

"Mine, too," Patrick said, patting his friend on the shoulder.

"I don't know," Alan said. "I could go for a bologna sandwich now."

The three boys looked at him with disgust.

No one noticed the sea serpent coming from the tunnel to their left. It came without making a sound. Its onyx arms extended outward, desperate, clawing. Before they could react, it had swallowed Chris in a deadly embrace.

"Chris!" Alan bellowed.

His brother tried to scream, but his mouth was crammed with oozing sea serpent flesh as it locked an arm over the lower half of his face.

It dipped its head down quickly, horrid mouth open wide.

Chris's skull cracked with a soul-shattering pop as the monster feasted on his brain. It sucked greedily while Chris's legs twitched and kicked. All three boys were hollering incoherently, shaken to their core as they watched their friend and brother get devoured.

Patrick had a little wasabi left in the container. He regained his senses and splashed it on the creature at the same time as Alan ran at it with a strangled cry, stabbing an arrow in its head, over and over again.

Chris dropped into the murky water, headless.

The sea serpent flipped onto its side, melting. It reached for Chris, but Alan stomped on its stunted arm. They could hear its bones crack. Chris's body lay on its back, water collecting on his side as if he were a dam.

"Help me get him up," Alan said, sniffling back tears.

It wasn't easy getting Chris's body out of the sewer, his blood pouring from his open neck cavity, splashing down on them as they hoisted him up the ladder.

When they emerged into the cooling dusk, they were surrounded.

Everyone in the town who had been hiding in their homes stood around the sewer, waiting for them. A huge cheer went up when they saw Patrick, then David. The boys flinched, taken off guard.

Their revelry was cut short when Alan came up, cradling his brother's headless body.

"Hey, everyone get out of here! This is private property!"

All heads turned to crab-ass Ernie. He carried a broom, as if he could sweep the crowd of thirty or more away.

Patrick hit David's chest with the back of his hand.

"Look."

A small sea serpent, what they hoped was a lone survivor, came up out of the other sewer grate across the street, just behind Ernie. No one warned their irritating neighbor it was there.

"I already called the cops!" Ernie shouted.

"Sure you did," David said.

The sea serpent latched onto the man's leg, eating the meat at the back of his knee. Ernie went down, crying in pain while the monster scrabbled up his chest, going for his throat.

Patrick walked through the crowd and shot it with the BB gun, three, four, five times. The little beast shrieked and fell off Ernie's chest.

"Leave us alone," Patrick said. "Forever."

Ernie yowled in pain, clutching his leg. "I need help! Somebody call an ambulance."

No one made to go in their house and make the call. They were too transfixed by the melting monster.

David said, "I think I'm too tired to feel bad for Ernie."

"Yeah, me too," Patrick said.

A car, the first moving car they'd seen in hours, came down the street slowly.

Patrick dropped his BB gun. He ran to the driver's side door.

"Mom!"

She rushed out, tears cascading down her face, and wrapped her arms around him. Patrick didn't feel the least bit like a baby, hugging his mother and crying into her neck while the whole neighborhood watched. He thought he'd lost her. He never wanted to let her go.

"I came just as soon as the police opened the barricades. I was so worried about you."

"D…D…Dad," was all he could manage to croak out.

She hugged him harder.

"I'm so sorry I left you. I just wanted to get a few things."

He stared at her face, still numb to the fact that she was here. "It's okay, Mom. There was no way to know this was gonna happen."

He noticed David standing by his mother's car, peering in the window. He motioned for Alan to come over.

"What is it?" Patrick asked David.

David shook his head slowly. "No way."

Patrick reluctantly broke from his mother's embrace and stepped to the car. He saw the box lying on the back seat and gasped.

THE AMAZING SEA SERPENTS! FUN FOR THE WHOLE FAMILY! JUST ADD WATER!

"Mom, where did you get that?"

She rubbed her hand on his back, sniffling back tears. It seemed as if everyone was now gathered around the car in breathless silence. "I found it at KG Toys. I remember how much you wanted them, so I was going to surprise you."

The blood in Patrick's veins turned to ice. He looked to his friends, who couldn't stop staring at the Amazing Sea Serpents box.

"David, you have a big grill in the yard. Get as much coal and lighter fluid as you can."

His mother grew confused. "What are you talking about, Patrick?"

He opened the door and grabbed the box.

"We have to burn this first. I'll tell you everything...after I'm sure there's nothing left."

David said, "Mrs. Richards, were there other sea serpent kits in the store?"

"Yes. A whole shelf of them."

Patrick shivered.

There were going to be a lot of fires tonight.

# Optical Delusion

*For a man who truly gets it, Jim Herbert. And I'm sure he has his own pair of X-ray specs.*

# Chapter One

If there was one thing Martin Blackstone truly hated, it was being disturbed during the two hours he allowed himself a night to watch television. After working all day at the factory, was it too much to ask for two goddamn hours of peace and quiet?

Especially tonight, *Charlie's Angels* night.

Even Andrea knew not to bother him when *Charlie's Angels* was on. All his buddies wanted a piece of that Farrah, but Blackstone had never been into blondes, no matter how pointy their nipples were poking out of red bathing suits on posters. No, he was a Jaclyn Smith man. That girl was specially handcrafted by God himself. He'd never kick her out of bed for eating crackers, that was for sure.

Not that his wife was some slouch. Back in her prime, she could turn heads with the best of them. She was still attractive, but *mommy-attractive*. Jaclyn Smith was on a whole different level. He bet she'd be hot even when she was in her seventies.

*Whump, thump!*

"Keep it down up there!" he shouted at the ceiling.

The Angels were running. He daren't take his eyes off the tube. Unfortunately, it wasn't one of those slow-motion shots.

"It's just the boys having a little fun," Andrea said, crocheting yet another baby blanket. Blackstone often wondered if any of their neighbors knew about the miracle of condoms. It seemed someone was coming up pregnant every month. Crazy Italian Catholics. Here they were, having all kinds of irresponsible fun, none of them thinking how it kept his wife doing hard labor, crocheting blanket after blanket like an enslaved seamstress.

"They can have fun without breaking through the floor."

Andrea waited until the commercial to speak again. "Brian's been cooped up all week. He needs to blow off a little steam."

Blackstone shook his empty beer can. Andrea got up to get him another.

"The kid had all day to get it out of his system." He popped the leg-rest up on his brand-spanking-new lounger. It was so comfortable that on some nights, he started fights with Andrea just to have an excuse to come downstairs and sleep on it.

"Noel had school, then he had to go home and do his homework and wait for dinner. Brian was practically jumping out of his skin waiting for him to get here." She handed him a cold Schaefer. They said it was the one beer to have when you're having more than one. Blackstone could testify to that. He pulled the top back and dropped the ring in the ashtray. The cold beer chilled him all the way down to his softening belly.

They heard muffled laughter, followed by what sounded like his sixteen-pound bowling ball being dropped to the floor. "If they don't settle down, I'll chuck their asses outside."

Andrea snatched up her blanket and dropped into the chair next to him, bristling. "You'll do no such thing. It's pitch-black and cold out there. You want Brian to get sick again?"

His irritation deflated and he sighed. "No, of course I don't."

Brian had just gotten over a hell of a case of chicken pox. He had more bumps on his skin than a West Virginia highway. They had to put socks over his hands to stop him from scratching and popping the sores. Being a ten-year-old, he was not enthralled with their solution. The doctor and medication had cost a pretty penny. The last thing Blackstone wanted to do was add a visit to one of those skin doctors to the ledger, so he'd told him to suck it up.

The socks were off now and Brian was feeling good enough to go back to school on Monday. His best friend Noel had been asking daily when he could come over.

Andrea patted his hand. "You may have had a bad day, but Brian has had a bad week."

"I know. All that talk about capping salaries has my blood boiling. That place is making money hand over fist and the greedy asshole owners want more. So how do they get it? By taking from the little guys. We got a meeting with union officials next week."

"The union won't let it happen. No sense giving yourself a stroke thinking about it."

"If there's a strike…"

He bit his tongue. Andrea was right. There was no reason to keep harping on it. There'd be plenty of time later if and when the shit hit the fan.

Blackstone tried to settle down, remembering what it was like when he was the same age. Then *Charlie's Angels* came back on with a close-up of Jaclyn Smith and all of his thoughts were derailed. He drank his beer and indulged in his weekly fantasies.

Before he knew it, the show was over and *Vega$* was getting ready to start.

"You have to walk Noel home," Andrea said.

Noel had been granted a special late curfew just this Wednesday because he'd missed his friend so much. Plus, tomorrow was a half day in school, some kind of teachers' special meeting. Not much schoolwork would be getting done. Noel only lived ten houses down the street, but somehow, Blackstone had been roped into walking the kid home tonight.

He drained the rest of his beer, went to the kitchen and dropped it in the garbage. He could still smell Andrea's chicken casserole. His stomach grumbled. Eyeing the refrigerator, he said, "I'll be back for you in a few." A couple of spoonfuls of cold casserole would soak up the booze and prevent a hangover.

Slipping a Schaefer in his pocket for the walk, he marched upstairs, Andrea saying, "Thank you, Marty," as he passed by the living room.

The door to Brian's bedroom was closed. There were drawings of space battles from *Star Wars* taped all over it. Blackstone stood there for a moment, admiring the latest one. It showed two X-wing fighters engulfed in flames spiraling into a nearby planet. The kid was good. Maybe he should get him to draw that turtle they always advertised to see if he could make it into art school.

The only flaw in the drawing was in the science of it. You can't have flames in space, Blackstone said to himself, chuckling. The shit he knew thanks to his subscription to *Popular Mechanics*. It was probably a good idea to encourage Brian to start reading it too. He'd be a man someday, and men needed to know all kinds of shit.

He opened the door without knocking. Brian's *Star Wars* figures were all over the floor. There was a cardboard box that had been cut up and pasted back together with etchings on the sides so it looked like the big garbage collector that the little Jawas rode around in, searching for scrap metal and droids.

Blackstone sighed again. There was way too much *Star Wars* trivia rolling around his head for his taste. It was all the kid talked about. They'd gone to the movies to see it five times. He couldn't remember ever seeing a movie five times, not even the ones he loved like *The Bridge on the River Kwai* or *The French Connection.*

He kept praying *Star Wars* would fade away and finally get pulled from the theater, but so far, God wasn't listening. Or if He was, He was taking great delight in Blackstone's suffering.

Brian and Noel were huddled together, making Luke and Vader have a lightsaber fight. The boys looked so much alike, it was scary. Same black hair, same bowl cut, both small for their age with knobby knees. No wonder they'd become inseparable.

"Okay guys, time for Noel to head on home."

The boys groaned, but he only smiled, shrugging as if to say, *Don't blame me, I didn't make the rules on this one.*

The cold Schaefers had definitely mellowed him a bit.

"Can't he stay for another half hour?" Brian said.

Blackstone tapped his watch. "Your mother promised he'd be home at ten. Come on, time's ticking."

Tonight's episode of *Vega$* was a rerun, so he didn't mind missing it. He could always catch the tail end of the CBS movie and zone out before heading up to bed.

"Fine," Brian said, chin on his chest.

Noel, who was always a chipper kid, said, "You want to see what I got for Brian, Mr. Blackstone?"

"Sure, but only if it doesn't take long."

"It won't." The boys pushed the toys and comics on the floor around, searching. Noel uncovered a pair of black glasses and handed them to him. "Glasses?"

Noel's perpetual smile widened. "More than that. They're X-ray glasses. I ordered them from a comic book weeks ago. They just came in the mail today. I got one for me and one for Brian."

The cheap plastic glasses were light as a feather. Blackstone expected to see the usual red spiral painted on the lens to give the illusion of something strange and mysterious happening to the wearer. These lenses were clear and dark, like sunglasses.

Brian said, "Yeah, but they don't really work. It kind of gave me a headache."

"That's because you have to get used to them. The manual said that the more you wear them, the deeper you'll see."

Blackstone chuckled. "Or more likely, you'll go cross-eyed. How much did they cost?"

"A dollar each."

He flipped the glasses onto the ruffled bed. "Well, at least you're not out a lot of money."

Noel got into his coat, tucking his own glasses in his pocket. "It kinda hurt my head too, but I'm going to stick with it."

"You know what they say: No pain, no gain." Before he left the room, he said to Brian, "Clean up this mess before your mother gets up here. She'll have a fit."

"I know."

*Yeah, he knows.* The kid spent half his life punished because he didn't do all the things he knew he should be doing. Blackstone just shook his head, leading Noel down the stairs.

"Good-bye, Mrs. Blackstone."

Andrea looked up from her baby blanket. "Good night, Noel. Thanks for cheering Brian up."

The walk to Noel's house was bitterly cold. The first snow of winter was coming soon. Blackstone could smell it. He dropped the kid off, exchanged a few pleasantries with Noel's father, who was the manager of a health-food store in the next town over, and headed back home. He took his time, sipping the beer along the way. Before he went inside, he dropped the beer can in the metal garbage pail outside. He didn't want Andrea riding his ass over his not being able to walk a single block without a beer.

She didn't understand. She had a pretty cushy life. Andrea didn't need a few beers to settle down so she could sleep.

As he walked in the door, she was coming down the stairs.

"He's already asleep. Guess he's not ready for prime time yet."

"Guess not. Well, he has four more days to get ready."

"You never had chicken pox, did you?"

He shook his head. "Chicken pox is afraid of me."

Andrea gathered her blanket and yarn and needles in a canvas bag, got up and kissed the top of his balding head. "I'm going up. Don't stay up too late. You don't get to stay home from school tomorrow."

"Don't remind me. I'm just gonna watch a little bit of the news."

He watched her leave in her baggy sweatpants and oversized shirt. He missed the days of lingerie or even better, birthday suits. Having a kid had a way of changing all that.

Another Schaefer would have been nice, but he made it a point not to drink a full sixer on weeknights. It helped make the weekend special. There was nothing good on TV, so he flipped through *Reader's Digest* until the eleven o'clock news. It started out with the latest namby-pamby nonsense being spewed by the president. Hearing anything about Jimmy Carter set his teeth on edge, so he decided to call it a night.

He peeked in on Brian, nestled so deep under his *Fantastic Four* comforter that only the top of his head was visible. His X-ray glasses were on the floor. Blackstone picked them up and put them on. He'd always wanted a pair when he was a kid, but his parents refused to get them.

The room darkened and it felt as if his eyes were being stretched. That was the only way he could describe it. A headache instantly bloomed around his forehead.

"Now, that's a look," Andrea said, shuffling down the hall to the bathroom in her puffy pink robe.

"X-ray specs," Blackstone said. "Noel bought a pair for Brian."

"They look like sunglasses, not X-ray glasses."

"Not that there's any such thing as X-ray glasses."

"Well, for what it's worth, they make you look kind of... cool. Like back when you used to wear those Wayfarers when we were dating."

The pain in his forehead skittered to his temples. Still, he kept them on. He couldn't remember the last time Andrea had said he looked cool.

"You want to cruise around in my Mustang?"

"I'll settle for our Buick."

She laughed, slipping into the bathroom.

But before she disappeared from view, Blackstone thought he saw something that shouldn't have been.

He could have sworn he caught a glimpse of her ratty pajamas under her closed robe.

# Chapter Two

Another day, another buck. Blackstone's sweat turned to ice the moment he stepped out of the boiling factory into the cold. Everyone's breath came out in great, thick clouds as they filed into the parking lot.

"You coming over for cards Saturday night?" Jack Fortman said. He tossed his metal lunch pail into his car, a Dodge Dart with black primer on two of the quarter panels.

"Does the pope shit in the woods? I'll bring beer and peanuts."

"Just don't get those ones in the shell that are salted. I gotta watch my blood pressure. Though I'm sure that union meeting will bring on full heart failure."

"Then you should try winning a hand every now and then."

"That's why I need to make sure you're coming," Fortman said, chuckling.

It took three cranks of the ignition to get the Buick started. Blackstone flipped the heat on full blast, trying to thaw out. There was an accident on I-98 going home, so a twenty-minute drive took over an hour.

The moment he walked in the door, Andrea was there to greet him. She took his coat and lunch pail and gave him a big kiss on the lips. "I heard about the traffic on the radio."

"Yeah, it was great."

She led him to the kitchen. "Here's a beer. I had to put dinner in the oven to keep it warm. I didn't know when you'd be home."

"Hey Dad," Brian said. He was eating from a foil TV dinner tray. They'd long given up the fight trying to get him to eat normal food. The kid had about four taste buds. TV dinners with veal cutlet, mashed potatoes and something they called a hot brownie accounted for three of them.

"Don't you ever get sick of that?"

Andrea put a chilled beer in his hands and went to the oven.

"Why would I?"

It was a good question. Brian knew the things he liked, and he could indulge in them every day without thinking about all the other stuff he could be missing. Blackstone sometimes envied his son.

"You couldn't at least wait for me?"

"I was starving."

He smelled the pot roast and roasted potatoes and his own hunger went into overdrive. Andrea could cook the holy hell out of a pot roast.

"Yeah, me too."

Dinner was a quiet affair. Andrea knew he needed time to unwind and with Brian home, there was no school to talk about. When Blackstone was done, he went upstairs to smoke a cigarette while he took his post-dinner shit. It was the little things in life that made getting up in the morning worth it.

Going to his bedroom to change, he saw the X-ray glasses on his bedside table. He'd put them there last night, but had forgotten, until now, that strange glimpse of his wife's pajamas under her robe.

"Must have been the beer," he said, picking them up. He put them back on and instantly, the headache returned. Again, there was that feeling of his eyes being pulled like taffy.

He turned around at the sound of footsteps.

"You like them, Dad?" Brian said.

"*Like* is a very strong word."

"You can keep them. They stink, but they do make you look like a policeman."

Blackstone grinned, pointing his finger at his son like a gun. "Freeze. You're under arrest. So, you thought you'd get away, didn't you?"

Brian held his hands up high, laughing. "I confess. I stole all the Swedish Fish at the corner store."

"I always knew I'd nab you, Swedish Fish bandit."

When he spied his alarm clock, he saw it was almost time for *Mork & Mindy*. A little mindless entertainment was exactly what he needed tonight, although Brian had done a good job taking the edge off.

"How about instead of jail, you get me a beer and some potato chips?"

"Okay."

Brian ambled downstairs. The one job he liked to do was getting his mother and father their drinks and snacks before TV time.

Blackstone plopped into his lounger, the beer and chips already on the table. He lit up a Marlboro and turned on the TV with the wired remote control.

"You wearing those things again?" Andrea asked.

"What?"

She pointed at his eyes.

"Christ, I forgot I had them on." The weird sensation must have worn off while he was goofing with Brian.

"How can you even see with them on?"

He stared at her standing by the grandfather clock. Everything looked a lot darker last night when he'd first tried them on. It wasn't so bad now.

"Cool guys don't need to see," he quipped, flipping to channel seven.

"Or crazy people."

When she moved to take her seat, Blackstone choked on his beer.

For just a split second, he was able to see her bra underneath her wool turtleneck!

And just like that, it was gone.

"You all right?" she said, patting his back.

Recovering, he said, "Just went down the wrong pipe."

He looked back at her, staring at her chest, though she couldn't tell behind the dark glasses. All he saw now was a sea of itchy wool.

"Are you going to watch TV with those things on?" she asked.

"Um, no, of course not." He took the glasses off, folded them and put them by the ashtray.

*Mork & Mindy* came on, but all he could think about was that brief, crystal-clear glimpse of Andrea's bra.

# Chapter Three

Fridays meant a quick stop at the Rusty Nail Saloon for a couple of cold ones with Jack Fortman and Joe "Holes" Metrano.

Holes didn't work at the factory. He, in his own estimation, was a professional gambler, betting on the ponies at the OTB. Most people knew him as "Holes in Head" on account of the dumb bets he made. The only reason he wasn't living in a cardboard box was because he still hung his clothes in the bedroom he'd grown up in. His mother made sure to take very good care of him.

"First round's on me," Holes said when he and Fortman grabbed a couple of stools at the bar.

"You must have hit," Blackstone said, holding up two fingers to the bartender. He still couldn't remember the guy's name—he'd only started a month ago—but the kid already knew which beer they preferred. Nothing beat an ice-cold Schlitz on tap.

"Got the exacta in the fifth at Aqueduct, then I hit a box triple in the seventh at Yonkers. I'm loaded, fellas."

Fortman snorted, guzzling half his beer down. "The payout couldn't have been that much. Unless you played one of your insane long shots."

Holes didn't let Fortman rain on his parade. "If that's the case, you can get the next round, working stiff."

They settled into their usual banter, bitching about the Giants, that pantywaist Carter, and the shit storm brewing at the factory. The Rusty Nail started to fill up, the happy-hour crowd pouring in for cheap drinks and pickled eggs.

After a couple of beers, Fortman announced with a burp that he had to take a piss.

"I think I'll join you," Holes said.

"What are you, some kinda woman? Guys don't go to the bathroom together," Fortman protested.

"They do when they both have to take a leak. Marty, order another round and tell him to put it on my tab. You're nice, so you get a free ride tonight."

Blackstone laughed, wagging a finger at Fortman. "See, being mean doesn't pay."

Fortman flipped him the bird and angled through the crowd, Holes on his heels.

Reaching into his pocket, Blackstone retrieved the plastic X-ray specs. He brought them hoping for a moment like this. What better way to truly test them than at a bar full of good-looking chicks? It was one thing to sneak a peek at Andrea's bra. He'd seen that and everything underneath more times than he could count.

Now, if they really worked, and he wasn't losing his mind, this was going to be his finest hour at the Rusty Nail. He just had to do it fast before the guys returned and wondered why the hell he was wearing sunglasses inside.

He slipped them on, blinked hard twice and sucked in a deep breath as his eyeballs wobbled in their sockets. It was so disturbing, he almost ripped them right off.

Then a pretty redhead—who couldn't have been older than twenty-four—sauntered by. She didn't even notice him, but he couldn't help but see the black panties she wore under her skirt.

His heart jumped.

His eyes stayed glued to her panties until she disappeared into the crowd. *Holy shit, it really works!*

Scanning the crowd, he spotted a smiling brunette with long, feathered hair. She was sipping what looked to be a Manhattan, standing by one of the small round tables along the side of the tavern. His eyes traveled down from her smile to the frilly bra under her black shirt. He'd look down even lower, but his view was blocked by the table and a guy sitting opposite her. A quick attempt to see her panties resulted in a clear view of the guy's tighty-whities.

Blackstone slammed his eyes shut, turning away.

It was just as well, as he spotted Holes walking back. He quickly took off the glasses and jammed them in his pocket.

"You lose Jack?"

"That guy pisses like a broken faucet. He may be there until last call."

Fortman eventually returned and they had one last beer, knowing they were going to see each other again tomorrow at poker.

It was dark out when Blackstone got to his car. He put on the glasses. Damn, too dark to see. He couldn't drive with them on.

It would have been nice to see what he could glimpse walking the streets, though. Plenty of people were out, ambling from bar to bar.

There was always tomorrow.

"How the hell are these things working?" he said over and over on the drive home. He'd have to consult the pile of back issues of *Popular Mechanics* this weekend. Maybe there was something in there that touched on some breakthrough development in X-ray technology that he'd somehow glossed over.

\* \* \* \*

"You have a nice time?" Andrea said.

"Just peachy," he replied, putting his coat in the closet.

"Pizza's in the oven. I'll get you a slice. You want meatball or sausage and onions?"

"One of each."

He settled into his chair. Friday nights were a whole different ritual. Pizza night meant Andrea and Brian ate early, not waiting for him to return from the Rusty Nail on account of some Fridays, he didn't get home until it was technically Saturday.

As Andrea walked into the kitchen, he put on the X-ray specs. Hmmm, she was wearing her special panties with the lace edges. He knew what that meant. Blackstone felt his skin flush with anticipation. It was kinda nice knowing what was to come.

The glasses were tucked between his leg and the chair's cushion before she returned with his pizza.

"Just let me know if you want another slice," she said, her fingers brushing the hair behind his ear.

Drinks with the boys, ogling strange women's underwear, pizza and now a little Friday-night boogie in the bedroom.

What had he done to deserve this?

And what was Noel seeing with his glasses? Blackstone made it a point to make sure the kid never wore them while he was in the house. He didn't need that twerp salivating over Andrea.

# Chapter Four

Saturdays were always a rough start.

The only good thing about waking up with a hangover was knowing the day could only get better as it moved along.

Blackstone was having a tough time seeing the bright side of things at the moment. He woke up to a jackhammer in his skull, mouth dry as confetti, stomach feeling like it had up and died. That damn woodpecker was banging away on the dead tree in the yard again, each strike of its beak a spike in Blackstone's skull.

"Drop dead already," he murmured into his pillow.

Reaching a hand out, he felt Andrea's side of the bed empty. He dared to open one eye and saw it was past eleven. He had to take a piss but was having a hard time willing his body up and out of the bed. Eventually, the desire not to wet the sheets like a baby trumped the need to burrow under them and not move a muscle for a few more hours.

After a quick pit stop, he shuffled downstairs to the smell of bacon. Brian sat in front of the TV, watching cartoons: *Road Runner*, to be specific. Blackstone got a kick out of *Road Runner*. Normally, he'd sit and watch it with Brian, but not today. Not when he was feeling like a dog that had been run over flat by a semi.

"Shouldn't you be sweeping?" he grumbled.

Sweeping around the outside of the house was Brian's solitary chore on Saturday mornings. It was now almost noon and the kid was still zoning out in front of the TV.

His son looked at him with barely concealed horror. Blackstone had seen his reflection in the bathroom mirror and couldn't blame him.

"I was going to do it after *Looney Tunes*."

Blackstone twisted the knob on the TV, shutting it off just as Road Runner was about to light a bomb under Wile E. Coyote's ass.

"Show's over. Sweep and go find your friends. Come home when your mother calls you for dinner."

Brian gave an exaggerated sigh, stomping past him.

"And no bringing anyone over here to play," Blackstone added.

He jumped at the touch on his shoulder.

"Someone's chipper today."

Andrea carried a loaded laundry basket. Her hair was tied up under a bandanna.

"Is there coffee?" he asked.

"As my husband would say: 'Does the pope shit in the woods?' There's leftover bacon on the table too."

He mumbled something that might have been a thank-you. Even he wasn't sure.

"Good thing we had our fun before you finished all that beer," she said.

It sure had been fun. Blackstone, knowing she had her sex panties on ahead of time, had been ready and waiting. By the time Brian fell asleep and Andrea moved to sit on his lap, he was ravenous.

He squeezed her butt cheek before shuffling to the kitchen.

"Maybe we can try again tonight."

She ruffled his hair. He thought his skull might shatter into bits. "We'll see. Right now, I don't think you could handle it."

As she went up the stairs to put away the clothes, Brian passed her, running outside and avoiding eye contact with his father. He slammed the door behind him. Blackstone heard the garage door open, then the sweet sound of Brian sweeping the front steps.

He'd always hated sweeping himself, which was why he delegated that chore to his son a year ago in exchange for his allowance. That allowance afforded Brian a slice of pizza at Willie's Pizzeria and an afternoon of pinball. He thought it was a pretty fair exchange.

Grabbing a cup of coffee and loading bacon on a buttered roll, he opened one of the living-room windows a crack and sank into his lounger, letting the cool air wake him. He felt something jab his leg, saw it was the X-ray specs.

He almost put them on, but wasn't sure his hangover headache could handle the X-ray specs eye yank. He waited until he ate his breakfast, had another cup of coffee and a glass of water to wash down two aspirin. Andrea was upstairs, singing "Maria" from *West Side Story*, cleaning the bathroom.

Standing at the kitchen sink, he looked out into their small, perfectly square yard. His neighbor, Frannie, was outside watching her poodle run around. Frannie was a recent divorcée who'd moved into the downstairs apartment in the house behind them a year ago. She was pushing forty but looked thirty, with long auburn hair and a cigarette perpetually between her full lips.

Blackstone went back to the lounger and grabbed the glasses.

"Well, hello there."

It looked like Frannie had decided not to wear a bra today. Her small breasts were still pert despite the years, nipples puckered from the cold.

He looked over the glasses, and saw she was wearing a thin coat over her sweater. Smoke hung over her like a cloud. Then he looked through the glasses to stare at her tits until she turned around and took her poodle inside.

"Now that's a sure hangover cure."

Taking the glasses off, he winced as the arms pressed on the sides of his head. His face must have been swollen from all the drinking. Massaging the bridge of his nose, he went to the basement bathroom to take a hot shower. He needed to fix one of the kitchen cabinets today and he had to bounce back so he could play poker later tonight.

And maybe he'd take a stroll around the block with his X-ray specs, just to do some further scientific testing.

\* \* \* \*

"I'm heading to the corner store to get a pack of cigarettes. You need anything?"

"We could use some butter and a can of tomato soup," Andrea said. She'd finally taken a break, sitting at the kitchen table flipping through a magazine, piping-hot coffee close at hand.

"Butter. Soup. Got it." Blackstone put on his winter coat, making sure the glasses were in his pocket.

"Good work on the cabinet," Andrea said before he walked out the door. "I knew I kept you around for something."

"You keep doing what you did last night and I'll stay around."

He heard her snicker as he closed the door, a gust of cold air blasting him in the face. The weatherman said it would snow on Monday. Asshole was usually wrong. Felt more like snow on Sunday to Blackstone.

Walking up the street to the corner store, he put the X-ray specs on. The bright day got a little duller, but not as dark as the glasses made things just the day before. He really didn't need more cigarettes. He still had half a carton in the basement. But he needed an excuse to walk around.

Because of the cold, the block was quiet. No matter. This wasn't about seeing more boobs and underthings, though that would have been a bonus. He knew that already worked.

No, now it was on to even bigger things.

He paused outside Mr. Otello's house, a two-family brick behemoth the old man kept meticulously. Blackstone stared hard at the first floor of the house. After ten seconds, all he could see was brick. He tried the door. The wood grew fuzzy for a moment, but he couldn't see past it.

So much for that, Blackstone thought.

A few houses away, he stopped beside a metal mailbox secured to the fence outside Mrs. O'Hanlon's yard. This time, he was able to peer through the thin aluminum and see the stack of mail and folded magazines inside.

"Maybe the material can't be too thick."

He spotted some cardboard in Mrs. O'Hanlon's garbage. Walking past the fence, he plucked the cardboard out and placed it in front of the statue of the Virgin Mary she'd put next to her birdbath. It only took a few second to laser right through the cardboard. He could easily see the crack in Mary's face from the time Steve Liebert walloped it with an errant football.

Hoping Mrs. O'Hanlon hadn't seen him rooting through her garbage and messing with her holy statue, he dashed out of the yard.

"Hey Martin. Can you do me a favor?"

Willie Riley startled him.

Somehow, the neighborhood's octogenarian had managed to sneak up on him like an Indian tracker.

"Oh, hi Willie. What was that?"

"You heading to the corner store?"

Blackstone made the mistake of looking at the man, dressed in tan slacks that had seen better days and an old peacoat that had more holes than a wedge of Swiss cheese. In a flash, he saw right down to the man's stained underwear, the yellow ring around his flaccid penis revolting enough to make Blackstone stagger.

"You all right?" Willie said.

Blackstone whipped the glasses off.

"Yeah. Nursing a hangover."

That brought a smile to Willie's face. "I wish I could drink enough to *get* a hangover. It's too cold for me to walk up there, but I really need milk, salami, and a loaf of bread. You think you could get it for me? Here's five dollars. You can even keep the change."

Blackstone shivered, not from the cold, but from the horror of what he'd just accidentally seen. The last thing he wanted was to be everyone's errand boy, but you didn't say no to Willie when he asked for a little help.

"Sure, Willie, sure. Except you're getting your change. Boss said I'm not allowed to take tips."

Willie laughed, slapping his back. "Thanks a lot, Martin. You're a good kid."

No more testing for now, Blackstone thought, hands in his pockets as he rushed to the corner store. These glasses giveth, and they certainly taketh away.

# Chapter Five

"What'll it be, fellas? A little five-card stud or seven-card draw?" Fortman shuffled the cards, an unlit cigar crammed in the corner of his mouth. Blackstone, Holes, Harry Rondo and Benny Hartman from the factory sat around the kitchen table. Cold cans of Schaefer sat next to each fresh pile of chips, cigarette smoke filling the room.

"I'm feeling five-card stud," Holes said.

"Seven-card draw it is," Fortman said, the guys laughing. It was always best to go with the opposite of whatever Holes said.

"Who the heck do you think you are, Greta Garbo?" Rondo said, gesturing at Blackstone's glasses.

Blackstone had already crafted the perfect lie on the ride over.

"Had my eyes dilated at the optometrist. He said I have to keep these on for the rest of the day."

"You're gonna make me feel bad, taking money from a blind guy," Hartman said.

"I won't," Fortman said, dealing out the cards. "All right, feed the kitty and let's play."

When everyone lifted their cards, careful not to let the person next to him see, Blackstone nearly yelped with excitement.

Playing cards were thin, so he knew he'd be able to see through them. But he worried that he'd see *right through them* and not be able to make out what was printed on the other side. The moment he spied the pair of deuces in Holes's hands, he dropped all concern that tonight would be a bust.

*Just be patient*, he reminded himself.

He let Fortman win the first hand, as well as the second. Their host crowed like he was some kind of Vegas big shot. Holes took the next hand with a full house, queens over fours. Blackstone stayed in despite only having a pair of jacks. He'd seen *The Hustler* a few times and knew how to play this. And he was pretty sure the guys wouldn't break his hands at the end of the night.

Despite knowing every card being played in every hand, he let a half hour go by before making his move. Seeing that Rondo was bluffing with only a pair of sevens, Blackstone ran up the pot, trumping him with three nines. From that point on, he made it a point to win one out of every three hands, always getting the guys to throw a little more money in the pot.

Two hours later, Holes folded for the night, tossing his cards in disgust. "That's it, I'm tapped."

Hartman belched, chugging the dregs of his beer. "Me too. Looks like tonight was your night, Marty."

"Guess I was due."

Rondo hit his arm with the back of his hand. "Hell, you were overdue. I was starting to look at you as my personal bank, withdrawals only." He guffawed, cashing in his few remaining chips.

Only Fortman didn't laugh. He knew he'd counted his chickens before they'd hatched, and he was none too happy about the turn of events.

As Holes slipped into his coat, he said, "Maybe next time I should get my eyes dilated. Maybe they'll give me a pair of X-ray glasses. Right?"

Blackstone burst out coughing, choking on a good lungful of Marlboro red. It took him a moment to realize Holes was only kidding, not outing him.

Of course he was. *How the hell would he know I have actual X-ray specs*, Blackstone thought, shaking the man's hand as he walked out.

"I'll give you my eye guy's number," he joked.

* * * *

At last night's card game, Blackstone had made sure not to drink too much. He wanted to be up bright and early to continue with his experimentation. For once, he got up before Andrea and even Brian, creeping down the stairs, clutching the glasses.

Over orange juice and toast, he marveled at the X-ray specs. There was no way in hell they should work. The technology of 1978, he was damn sure, wasn't up to the point of being able to peddle such a miracle for a buck. Or even a million bucks.

After breakfast, he went to the basement, zeroing in on the leaning stack of *Popular Mechanics* magazines. He'd been a subscriber ever since he was a kid and held on to every issue. His logic was that sooner or later, the

Reds were going to drop a nuke on America. Within the pages of those magazines were the blueprints on how to build things. The survivors—and he planned to be one of them—would need that knowledge more than cash or gold if they wanted to crawl out from under the rubble and thrive.

Sitting in the old shop chair, he grabbed the one at the top and scanned the table of contents, looking for any articles on X-rays. He was twenty or so issues in when the floorboards creaked overhead.

"You down there, Marty?" Andrea said.

"Just working on a couple of things. Thought I'd get an early start."

"That's good. You want to come to church with Brian and me?"

He couldn't help but hear the note of hope in her voice.

"Not a chance," he replied. "Nice try, though."

He heard her walk to the kitchen, resigned to the fact that her husband was a heathen.

The next issue had a brief side article on advances in hospital X-ray protection for technicians, but not quite what he was looking for.

Then a terrible idea came to him.

Setting the magazine aside, he bounded up the basement steps. Andrea was poking a spoon in a grapefruit, the radio on low.

"On second thought, I think I will come," he said.

Her face brightened. "Really?"

He made sure to rub his right eye, reddening it. "Yeah. You finally wore me down."

"I might have to wear my special dress to mark the occasion. Hey, what's wrong with your eye?"

Blackstone leaned against the wall. "Ah, I probably got some grit in it from sanding some wood. Hurts like hell. Think I'll try to rinse it out, see if that helps."

"Okay, but we need to be ready to leave in half an hour. Brian's already up, brushing his teeth."

"I'll be ready. Hope the place doesn't get struck by lightning."

"There's a very strong possibility."

He went up to change, rubbing his eye until it hurt.

There'd be a lot of women in church, all packed into one place. What he was praying for was definitely not on God's approval list.

# Chapter Six

The last time Blackstone had been to church had been at his wedding twelve years ago. He'd been so drunk standing on the altar that he barely remembered any of it.

Sitting in the middle pew with the organ blasting, the lady next to him belting out one of the single most maudlin hymns ever conceived, he wished he'd popped a few beers before coming.

He made it a point not to look at the rotund church lady, at least not through the glasses.

Now, the cutie two rows up wearing the black lace bra and panties—that was another story. In fact, the entire congregation was laid bare to him. He just had to be careful where he looked.

Andrea gave his hand a gentle squeeze, looked up and smiled at him. He smiled back, seeing she'd worn her plain church bra, the cheap one that was all about function, not form. It covered her chest like an umpire's protective vest.

Even Brian was beaming, happy to finally have his father included in the misery, Blackstone surmised.

"In the name of the Father, and of the Son, and of the Holy Spirit," the priest intoned in a high singsong.

"Amen," everyone but Blackstone replied. After a few rambling prayers, they sat.

"Your eye feeling any better?" Andrea whispered, leaning into him.

"A little. The glasses are keeping the lights from making it worse," he lied. But it was a lie told in the interest of science.

At least that's what he'd convinced himself.

Everything about this was so bad. It was one thing to look through women's clothes around the neighborhood. Even a lapsed Catholic like him saw the depravity of being a Peeping Tom in a church, surrounded by his wife and son.

*What the hell is wrong with me?* he thought, listening to a woman with a stutter give the first reading. *Why can't I help myself? I'm no saint, but this is ridiculous. Maybe I should just cut it out and take the damn things off.*

His fingertips grazed the glasses when a new development presented itself. He happened to be looking down at the back of the pew. Only now, he was able to see through the wood to the flowered underpants of the nun sitting in front of him. Fascinated—not at the nun's choice of underwear, but that he could now see through the much thicker wood—he left them on.

Blackstone didn't hear a single word that was said for the rest of the Mass. He just kept looking around, seeing things that titillated him and others than made him cringe. He was especially astonished when, staring at the altar, he was able to penetrate through the thick slab of granite, then the priest's robes and pants. The second the Fruit of the Looms came into focus, he shifted his gaze, settling on a buxom woman across the aisle.

By the time the closing hymn was sung, he was light-headed.

Andrea snapped him back to reality when she patted his hand. "See, that wasn't so bad, was it?"

"No, I can't say that it was."

"And the church didn't burn down," Brian added, chuckling. "Can we go to the bakery now?"

Blackstone walked down the aisle, eyes glued to the bottom of a woman who had come to church naked as a jaybird under her polyester pantsuit. It wasn't much of an ass, but he'd been married so long, he was like a starving man feasting on an all-you-can-eat buffet.

"Earth to Marty," Andrea said, looping her arm in his.

"Huh?"

"Will you take us to the bakery? I want to get one of those crumb buns," Brian repeated.

"Yeah, sure, sure. Crumb buns."

All during the drive to the bakery, he found he could see through the metal of the cars around them, catching quick glimpses of folks in their skivvies. By the time they left the bakery, even underwear had become transparent. It was like walking around a nudist colony, except everyone was bundled up in the frigid air.

"Think I'm gonna take a nap," he said when they got home.

"Jesus can wear a man out," Andrea joked.

He ignored her, heading upstairs.

Holy cripes, he thought, sitting on the edge of his bed. That was... incredible.

He wasn't lying about needing a nap. The morning had sapped him of all his energy. Laying back on his pillows, he almost forgot to take off the glasses. They pinched his temples something fierce, almost hurting when they slid off. The brightness of the bedroom stung his naked eyes. He slammed his lids shut, the phantom feeling of the glasses still pressing on the sides of his head while he fell into a restless sleep.

\* \* \* \*

When he awoke, Brian was in his room with the door open, reenacting one of the scenes from *Star Wars* with his landspeeder skipping across the carpet. Despite the two-hour nap, Blackstone still felt tired...and achy. His temples and the bridge of his nose felt especially sore.

"Hey," he said, breaking up Brian's running commentary as he talked Luke Skywalker through the desert of Tatooine.

"Hi Dad. You want to play? You could be the sand people."

"Nah, not now. I've got a headache. I wanted to ask you: Where did Noel get those X-ray glasses?"

"From a comic-book ad."

"Can you show me?"

"Yeah. They have them in like every issue."

Brian opened up a dresser drawer that had been converted to his comic-book storage space. It was packed with four neat stacks of comic books. Blackstone saw covers for *Silver Surfer*, *The Avengers*, *Green Lantern* and *The Amazing Spider-Man*. He handed him a new issue of *X-Men*.

"The ads are always near the back."

Blackstone flipped through the comic, marveling at the level of artwork. Comic books had come a long way since he was a kid. He saw a guy with claws coming out of his hands cutting a robot in half. Crazy shit.

He found the adjust before the last page. It was a full-page listing of all kinds of cheap, useless crap that kids could pester their parents for, only to be disappointed when they were delivered ten to twelve weeks later.

In it were offers to learn karate in just four short lessons, a six-foot glow-in-the-dark monster ghost that could float in the air, a thousand soldiers complete with tanks and fighter jets, a hypnotism coin, and even a diamond ring for only twenty dollars.

But the centerpiece of the ad was the Scientific Wonder X-Ray Glasses. There was a picture of a man wearing the plastic sunglasses, looking through the wall of a house at the silhouette of a woman. The caption beneath it read: *It seems impossible, but see for yourself! You'll never look at the world the same way again. Great at parties. Fun for hours! Send a self-addressed, stamped envelope and $1 to Honor & Smith Co., PO Box 232, Minneapolis, MN. Money-back guarantee!*

"I really thought they'd work," Brain said. "I keep telling Noel he should write to them and get his money back, just like it says in the ad."

Blackstone closed the comic. "Odds are, they'll never even open the letter, much less send him his two bucks back. Them's the breaks, pal. These places are run by scam artists."

At least he used to think that.

"Well, at least they make good sunglasses, right?"

"At least they do that. Yep. I'm going downstairs to watch some TV. Carry on, Luke Skywalker."

He didn't realize until he'd gotten to the couch that he still had the comic in his hand. And he wondered what the Honor & Smith Co. would say if he told them what he'd been seeing with their gag gift. He bet they'd pay him a hell of a lot more than a buck to get their hands on them.

"What did you do to your face?"

Andrea sat next to him on the couch, gingerly touching his temples.

Blackstone flinched, backing away from her touch. "What do you mean? I just got up from my nap."

"I think those glasses are too tight. You have deep red depressions on the sides of your head and your nose. I don't think you should wear them again. Looks painful."

He got up and went to the mirror over the TV console. She was right. It almost looked like someone had drawn a partial outline of the X-ray specs on his face with a red pen.

"See?" Andrea said.

"I'll live." He plopped back down on the couch.

"Maybe I should throw them out."

"Just leave them be," he said, harsher than he'd intended. Andrea shrank away from him, clearly upset.

"Fine. It's *your* face."

She opened up a magazine while he turned on the TV. Neither of them said another word for the next hour.

# Chapter Seven

The weatherman was right for a change. By Monday morning, the first snow of the season had started to fall. They were only supposed to get a few inches, not enough to close school, which deflated Brian's hopes for one more day at home.

The factory would have been open even if there'd been two feet. The Buick slid all over the road, barely able to get traction on the slick blacktop.

Blackstone caught flak from Fortman about Saturday night, with a half-hearted accusation of cheating thrown in for good measure.

"Why the hell would I cheat?"

"Maybe because you were sick of having your ass handed to you."

"You're just upset that I pissed on your little victory dance."

Fortman shook his head. "Yeah, maybe just a little. I need a new snow blower. Got my eyes on this one at Sears. I thought Saturday night I'd have the dough to get it."

"Maybe next snowstorm. You wouldn't need it for this one anyway."

The whistle blew and it was time to get back to work. Blackstone had the X-ray specs in his coat pocket back in his locker. He planned to go into town for a bit before heading home. There was a very particular place he had in mind to visit.

Come quitting time, he made a beeline for his locker, practically running to his car. The snow had tapered off, but left a mess on the Buick that took time to clear off. He'd forgotten his gloves, so his hands were numb blocks of ice by the time he was done.

Gunning the engine, he checked his watch.

Got fifteen minutes to get there, he thought, goosing the accelerator to prevent the cold engine from stalling.

The roads had been salted while he'd worked, so the drive was far less treacherous. The normally bustling streets were much lighter on traffic, which only helped him get to Main Street faster. He pulled in next to a meter, ignoring the little *time expired* flag.

Stepping out into the bitter cold, he looked across the street at the squat building that was home to the real-estate office. There was a lone window with the blinds drawn.

Stacy Michaels worked in there. She was, by far, the single most attractive woman in the entire town, if not the state. He'd heard rumors that she was Miss New Mexico ten years back, before moving east and settling into a non-pageant life. She was as bright as she was beautiful and could sell a house like no other.

Every man Blackstone knew secretly lusted after her. They tended to walk very slowly past the real-estate office when the blinds were open. He'd spotted her here and there around town, and every time she took his breath away. She was tall and stacked, with olive skin and hair so black and shiny, it was as if she were a raven turned human. It was almost impossible to tear his gaze from her sparkling cobalt eyes and full, ruby lips. Catching her eye in the supermarket once, he'd actually walked right into the automatic door before it opened. It was embarrassing as hell, especially the way she quickly flicked her gaze away, snickering at the doofus who couldn't walk straight.

He wasn't alone in wondering what she looked like under those smart business clothes.

And now, at this very moment, even from across the street, she was going to be his. There was no way he was ever going to have a shot with her. Besides, despite everything that had been happening lately, he was a happily married man. A bit of a grouch at times and he often wondered how Andrea put up with him. It was one of the reasons he could never betray her.

Was this betrayal?

Hardly.

It was science, pure and simple. He was a pioneer, exploring the next step in the evolution of sight.

With shaking hands, he put the glasses on. A flake of snow landed on the left lens. He quickly wiped it off.

Leaning against his car as if he were waiting for someone, he stared hard into the real-estate building. In seconds, the brick melted away. He saw a bald man sitting in a chair. Angelo Munson, the owner, handed over papers for him to sign.

Blackstone moved past them before their clothes dissolved.

And there she was.

Stacy Michaels had her back to him, searching for something in a file cabinet. Instantly, he could see past her skirt and blouse, savoring the view of her high-cut panties. Then she turned, and it was as if her breasts defied gravity, the bra disappearing but each wonderful globe sitting high on her chest.

Her nipples were round and thick and a chestnut brown.

Not for the first time, Blackstone wondered if she had some Spanish blood. Definitely something exotic flowed through her veins.

Her breasts swayed as she walked to her desk. His eyes traveled south and the shock made him weak in the knees.

She was completely shaved down there!

He'd never seen anything like it, not even in magazines.

"Oh my God."

Here he prayed, not in church the day before.

Blackstone's heart danced, the whoosh of his pulse loud in his ears. He was still as a statue, refusing to even blink, taking in every square inch of the beyond-lovely Stacy Michaels. He felt himself harden and was grateful for the long wool coat he'd worn.

She picked up the phone, this stark-naked Venus, sitting back in her chair, legs crossed so he could no longer view the wonder between them.

"I think I'm gonna have a heart attack," he murmured, holding on to the bitter parking meter to keep upright. "Stacy fucking Michaels."

"What's that?"

Again, Blackstone was startled. Whenever he wore the glasses, he was transported to another world. Could anyone blame him?

"I'm sorry?" he said to the woman dressed in a thick parka, holding two paper bags of groceries.

"My mistake," she said with a slight scowl. "I thought you said something to me."

She powered through the snow. He made sure not to linger on her retreating form, turning back to Stacy. Now she was typing something. He concentrated on her mahogany-tipped breasts. All of the nipples he'd ever seen in real life were varying shades of pink. This was boldly going where he had never gone before.

In a quick, painful flash, he saw something else besides her breasts. The twin mounds of perfection were replaced by something red and wet. Blackstone blinked, rubbing his eyes beneath the glasses.

When he opened them again, everything was back to normal. Well, the new normal, at least.

"What the hell was that?"

He looked at the time on the clock by the bank down the street, saw it was time to get his ass home. He took one last lingering look at Stacy before getting in the car. This would have to become a daily stop after work. It beat the hell out of sitting in a bar with Fortman and Holes.

Taking the X-ray specs off so he could drive, he yelped when he felt something tear from the side of his head.

"What the hell?"

A tiny patch of skin stuck to the arm of the glasses. He angled the rearview mirror down to inspect his head. Right next to his ear was a blood-red circle. When he touched it with a fingertip, a bolt of pain went from one side of his head to the other.

He cursed the glasses, dabbing the wound with a napkin he found in the glove compartment.

"Cheap piece of shit."

How could the Honor & Smith Co. invest so much into the lenses and stick them in a cheapo plastic frame that was obviously shrinking? Pretty soon, he might not be able to fit them on his face, and that would be a true tragedy.

"Unless this whole thing is a mistake. There's no way they're selling real X-ray specs for a dollar in the back of comic books. Someone at Honor and Smith Co. really screwed up."

Pulling away from the curb, his mind buzzed with ways to explain the fresh cut by his ear.

# Chapter Eight

Brian was the first to notice the cut near his ear when he sat down to dinner.

"I think you need a Band-Aid, Dad."

"Nah, it's nothing. I banged my head on my locker. No biggie."

Andrea placed his plate of spaghetti and meatballs in front of him and inspected the wound. "Brian's right. I'm sure you didn't clean it either."

He so wanted to tell them to just leave it the hell alone, but he wasn't in the mood to argue. The image of Stacy Michaels was still buzzing in his brain and he wanted to savor it.

"Eyah! Are you crazy?"

Andrea, cotton ball in hand, eyed him like he was a recalcitrant child. "That cut needs peroxide. When did you get your last tetanus shot?"

He jammed half a meatball in his mouth. "What does that matter?"

"Because I don't need you getting lockjaw. Now hold still."

The next couple of dabs hurt much less. She finished the job with a round bandage, the kind they used to cover corns.

"There. All better."

Crisis averted, Brian talked nonstop about his first day back at school and all of the homework he had to catch up on and who got detention last week for peeing on Matt Winters in the boys' room and which teacher let out a fart when she was at the blackboard, pretending it never happened despite the class breaking into uncontrollable laughter. The kid talked so rapid-fire without seeming to take a breath, Blackstone wondered if he had a hidden blowhole on the top of his head.

"Oh, and Noel was out sick today. You think I should call him later? Maybe he got my chicken pox."

"Leave him be," Blackstone said. "Probably has a cold and is eating soup in bed, getting waited on hand and foot."

"You can call him," Andrea said, nudging him under the table.

Brian's face brightened and he finally stopped talking, tucking into his spaghetti.

By the time Blackstone was done, he had a whopper of a headache. "Think I'm gonna lie down."

"You look pale. How hard did you hit your head? I hope you don't have a concussion."

"I don't have a damn concussion," he snapped. "My head just glanced off the edge of the locker door. Work was a bitch today and I'm just tired."

He got up from the table, the overhead light feeling like daggers stabbing into his eyes.

"Don't take a nap this late, or you'll never get to sleep," Andrea said, bringing his plate to the sink. There was a sharp edge to her tone. She didn't appreciate his reaction, but so what? She'd live.

"I just need some aspirin."

"Hey Dad, you want me to get your drink and stuff when *WKRP in Cincinnati* comes on?"

"We'll see."

Blackstone lumbered up the stairs, chewed two aspirin and slumped onto his bed.

Nothing comes for free, he thought, lying in the dark. You didn't think you could see Stacy Michaels nude as the day she was born and not have the universe find a way to make you suffer, did you?

No matter. It had been worth it.

\* \* \* \*

He woke up the next day feeling fine. Even the cut on his head had healed remarkably well. He could barely even see it.

Though he *could* see the shriveled bit of flesh on the X-ray specs. He scraped it off with his thumbnail while he was in the bathroom getting ready for work. Blackstone realized he was hiding the glasses the way he smuggled issues of *Hustler*. Oh, but this was so much better than what was in the pages of the smutty mag.

Again, right after work, he parked outside the real-estate office. Today, before her underwear faded from view, Stacy Michaels wore red satin panties and a matching bra. He was almost sorry to see them dissolve.

Almost.

At one point, she walked over to Munson's desk to show him something. When he stood up, the man's hairy, flaccid cock came into full view. Blackstone turned his head away so fast, he nearly gave himself whiplash.

When he did, he found himself looking at a matronly woman in her late fifties pushing a metal cart filled with bags. This time, there was no slow fade of her clothes. She walked toward him fully exposed in horrid clarity. What was under those layers of clothes was as far from the pages of *Hustler* as his ass was from the rings of Saturn.

"Oh, Jesus," he barked, holding up his hand to block the view. Except he could see through his hand, catching a brief glimpse of bones, and still not miss an inch of the woman's rippling body.

He bent over, shutting his eyes tight, hearing her mutter something unpleasant about him as she wheeled past.

"If you only knew, lady," he said, though too softly for her to hear.

Still hunched over, he opened his eyes. The concrete sidewalk liquefied until he could see the sewer tunnel underneath his feet.

Closing his eyes again, he straightened up, hoping that when he opened them again, Stacy would have moved away from Munson. He couldn't take another cock shot.

Opening them slowly, he let out a vaporous sigh of relief. Stacy was alone in the office for the moment, standing while on the phone in all her full-frontal splendor.

"Now that's more like it."

Because of the cold, Main Street was relatively empty, so he wasn't too worried about talking out loud to himself.

Then his vision went blurry, and two seconds later it refocused, except in place of Stacy's amazing body was a skeleton moving around the desk, lungs pulsating under the rib cage, heart hammering away, a stomach that seemed suspended in midair sitting squat over twisty intestines.

Stacy's eyeballs were gone, replaced by dark sockets where things squirmed.

Blackstone shouted something, moving away from his car until his back hit the plate-glass window of the travel agency.

He turned his head skyward, seeing nothing but slate-gray clouds. In a flash, he pierced the clouds, seeing the hidden, unbroken blue skies.

What had just happened?

Blackstone couldn't get his heart rate to settle down. Someone tapped on the window behind him. He didn't turn around, afraid of what he'd see. So he jumped in his car and sped away, slicing down Main Street, blowing through the red light.

When he went to take the glasses off, his fingers slipped free. The glasses remained on his face as if they'd been glued on.

As he drove, he could see through the thick steel of the cars down to the grinding pistons, passengers nothing more than sitting medical-school skeletons. It was like driving through a house of horrors. All that was missing were recorded shrieks and moans.

Although he was supplying his share of moaning.

His eyes felt like someone had squirted lemon juice in them. His head pounded. The arms of the glasses dug deeper into his temples with each passing second. No matter how hard he tugged on them, they wouldn't come off. Cursing and punching the dashboard, he drove without knowing where he was going.

He finally stopped at the front of the abandoned school on the edge of town. PS 27 had been left to rot after they found toxic levels of asbestos all throughout the entire prewar building. It had been big news when the kids were evacuated as if the place were on fire. It took the Department of Education weeks to assign the students to different schools.

Engine idling, he used both hands to try and rip the glasses free. They wouldn't budge. All it did was stretch the skin of his nose, cheeks, and temples to very painful limits.

"Get…the fuck…off of me!"

Yanking again, he stopped cold when he heard a tearing sound. It was a warning that if he applied one more pound of pressure, he was going to be very, very sorry.

He sat in the car breathing heavily, face throbbing, eyes watering and his head feeling as if that asshole woodpecker had been trapped inside. An acidic burp singed his throat. Vomit was close behind. He opened the door, spilling his breakfast and lunch all over the cracked asphalt.

To his revulsion, a crow landed by the vomit, head cocking inquisitively.

"Don't eat that," he pleaded, getting back in the car.

The sleek black body disappeared. In its place was a skittering mass of bones and pulp. It pecked at the chunks of his tuna sandwich. He groaned, eyes closed, trying not to throw up again.

With his eyes shut tightly, he tried again to remove the X-ray specs. It was as if the crummy plastic had melted onto his face. Was there some kind of industrial adhesive that had seeped from the cheap glasses onto his skin? That had to be it.

But that was only half the problem. With his head thrown back against the seat, he opened his eyes, peering right through the Buick's roof to the cloudy sky and beyond.

What the hell was he going to tell Andrea when he came home with sunglasses on? When he slept with them?

And how was he going to able to look at his wife and son when their insides were laid out before him, looking more like walking nightmares than his family?

# Chapter Nine

Andrea was busy in the kitchen when he got home. The skeletal image of his wife stepped into the doorway when she heard him come in. He felt his bile rise at the sight of entrails, juices flowing in her digestive tract, blood whooshing in her veins and arteries.

Swallowing hard, he said, "Where's Brian?"

"Upstairs doing his homework," she said with her skeleton mouth. It reminded him a little of that *Sinbad* movie where he had to swordfight all those skeletons. Except this wasn't the least bit amusing.

He dared to touch her arm, expecting to feel the squish of exposed meat and warm, sharp bone. Thank God she at least *felt* normal. He walked her into the kitchen.

"You can take your glasses off, you know," she said. "Or does your eye hurt again?"

Blackstone had to turn away just to get a merciful break from that awful face. Gritting his teeth, he looked back to her, staring at empty orbital sockets.

"That's what I wanted to talk to you about." He kept his voice low. He didn't want Brian to overhear this.

"What do you mean?" Andrea flopped a tea towel over her shoulder.

"The problem is...I can't get them off."

He heard her laugh, though there was nothing in her ghastly appearance that gave any sign she was smiling.

"I told you those things were too small for your head, Marty. Here, let me try."

Before he could stop her, she gripped the arms and pulled. His head craned forward, his nose almost touching where hers should be. He choked back a gag.

"Ow!"

He staggered back.

"They really are stuck," she said, coming toward him. It took all of his self-control not to coil away. He had to keep reminding himself that this was Andrea, his wife, the woman who had turned him on so much just a few nights ago that he'd blown his load twice.

"Don't you think I know that?"

He reached into the fridge and saw only freestanding liquids, the containers invisible to him now. He grabbed what he hoped was a can of Schaefer, pulled the top off and chugged it down before reaching for another.

"What happened? I don't understand. How can sunglasses get stuck on your head like that? It makes no sense."

Swallowing back half of the second beer, he said, "I think maybe whatever glue they used to put them together leaked out. It's the only thing that makes sense."

As if being able to see right through your skin makes perfect sense, he thought, wondering if he needed to add some scotch to the mix tonight.

"We have to get you to the emergency room. I'm sure they have something that can dissolve the glue."

He shook his head. "You know how much an emergency-room visit costs? Not a chance."

Andrea had to go to the stove to turn the flame down on the three pots of food she had been cooking. He was grateful for the space between them, even though he could still see more of her than he'd ever wanted.

"I'll go see Doc Herbert tomorrow."

"You can't go to work like that."

He snorted. "No kidding. I'll have to take a sick day. First time in five years. They can't give me any flack for that."

That also meant he'd miss the big union meeting. Suddenly, it no longer seemed so important.

Andrea sighed, leaning against the counter. "I don't know whether to laugh or cry."

If it was just about the glasses stuck to his face, he'd be inclined to laugh too. There was no way he could tell her the rest. She'd think he'd lost his marbles.

"I'll be all right. Not sure how comfortable I'll be sleeping in these damn things."

Although, if he drank enough, that should be an easy problem to fix.

When Andrea hugged him, he stiffened for a moment. Sucking up his revulsion, he wrapped his arms around her, even going so far as to kiss her grinning teeth, feeling but not seeing lips.

Just keep drinking, he said to himself.

"What do we tell Brian?" Andrea asked.

"We laugh it off and just tell him they got accidentally glued on. He'll be fine. If he seems upset, I'll just talk about *Star Wars* and derail him."

"What about *Star Wars*?"

Brian waltzed into the kitchen, sniffed the pot of boiling potatoes, poured a glass of water from the tap and sat in his chair.

The sight of his little fleshless boy nearly made Blackstone scream.

Instead, he said, "Your mother and I were just wondering when the next movie will come out."

Brian proceeded to talk about rumors of the sequel, never once mentioning the X-ray specs, even while they ate. Blackstone finished all of the Schaefer in the fridge by the end of the night, polishing off enough Johnnie Walker later to pass out in his lounge chair, away from Andrea. There hadn't been enough alcohol in the house to get him to sleep next to a pile of bones and exposed organs.

\* \* \* \*

"So, what seems to be the problem, other than the hangover you're hiding behind those sunglasses?"

Dr. Herbert had been the family quack for the past ten years. Pushing sixty, the corpulent but practical doctor had come to a few poker nights over the years and discounted his charges every now and then when he knew times were tough at the factory. Blackstone liked him a lot, though not like this, with his guts in full view, food being digested by sloshing fluids.

And he was partially right. He did have a whopper of a hangover.

"It's the sunglasses that are the problem," he said, fresh strip of sterile paper crinkling as he shifted on the examining table. "I can't get the damn things off."

"Now, that's a new one. And I thought I'd seen it all."

The doctor reached into his pocket for a pack of cigarettes with his bony hand. "You mind?"

"No. Go ahead."

It was bizarre, watching the smoke roil around his lungs before being expelled in a thin column up his throat and out of his mouth. Blackstone knew he'd never touch a cigarette again after witnessing it, not even on late nights in the bar when a Marlboro went with booze the way Stacy Michaels was synonymous with va-va-voom.

The image of the last time he'd seen her made him shudder.

"Got the chills?" Dr. Herbert said, first feeling his head, then sticking a thermometer in his mouth. "Now, let me see what we have here. Martin, what kind of glasses are these?"

It embarrassed the hell out of him to say it out loud, but there was no sense holding at least that part back. He pulled the thermometer from between his lips and said, "X-ray specs."

"X-ray specs?"

Another draw on the cigarette, smoke billowing and churning in the doctor's lungs.

"They're my kid's. I was goofing around and put them on. I think the cheap glue or whatever they used to make them got on my face."

Dr. Herbert daintily touched the bridge of the glasses. Blackstone slammed his eyes shut as the skeletal finger got close to his eyes.

"I wouldn't call it cheap glue if it works this well. How long did you have them on?"

"Not long," he lied. "But I guess long enough for this to happen."

The doctor tried to move them, but they stayed put. He reached behind Blackstone's ear to see if he could get a finger under the arm and pry them off, but to no avail. His breath smelled like coffee and cigarettes, his face too close to Blackstone's. Blackstone squirmed on the paper, making a hell of a racket.

"Well, whatever they used, it's solid. It's almost as if those glasses were welded onto your face, Martin."

"Tell me something I don't know," he said irritably. His head and stomach hurt and his mouth felt like he'd licked the sawdust off the floor of the Rusty Nail.

"I think I have a solution that will do the trick. Now, I just need to find where I put it." He rummaged through the cabinets in the cramped room, opening and closing glass doors. Or at least that was the way Blackstone remembered them. Now, the doors were invisible to him.

Dr. Herbert popped his head into the hallway. "Madge. You know where that glue solvent is?"

A woman's nasally voice replied, "I'll look for it. It's not in the examining room?"

"If it was, I wouldn't be asking you."

Madge was Dr. Herbert's cousin, a woman who would have been very much at home during the temperance movement. She went to mass every day, scowled at people doing anything she deemed immoral—including holding hands in public—and was an inveterate busybody. Blackstone couldn't stand her and suspected the doc felt the same, but she was family and his cross to bear.

"I'll apply a little of the solvent to a section of the glasses with a Q-tip. It'll be a kind of test area to make sure it works and your skin doesn't have an adverse reaction before we try for the whole megillah. X-ray specs." He couldn't help chortling.

Blackstone was tempted to tell him to knock it off, but held his tongue. If he was in the doc's shoes, he'd be doing the same thing. Plus, he needed the man's help. If he didn't get them off and stop seeing through everyone, he was going to become an alcoholic before slipping into insanity.

"Is this what you're looking for?"

Madge walked in, a thin bundle of sticks and diseased-looking entrails. Blackstone couldn't help slipping back on the table, the paper protesting.

Because with Madge, he was seeing something more. If he thought things were as bad as they could get, he was dead wrong.

As her bones and organs began to fade, they were replaced by something else: Something dark and twisting, like old motor oil infused with mercury. It filled every part of the outline of her birdlike body, red orbs glowing where her eyes should be.

It was like looking into the face of hell itself.

"Get away from me!" he shouted.

Dr. Herbert paused, the glass of solvent in his hand. "Martin, what's wrong?"

"Don't let her come in here."

"That's a fine thing to say, Mr. Blackstone," Madge said, her voice dripping with disdain. She'd never liked him either, which had always been fine with him.

She was beyond horrid to behold.

Everything about her spelled one solitary word: Evil.

Blackstone jumped off the table, stepping to the doctor's left, keeping him as a barrier between himself and the thing that was Madge.

"Martin, I need you to calm down," Dr. Herbert said.

Madge placed a hand on the doctor's shoulder, urging him to throw Blackstone out of the office.

"Don't let her touch you!"

"Martin, I need you to calm down right this instant."

"He's probably drunk," the Madge-demon said. "Let him go sleep it off somewhere. We have *real* sick people waiting to see you."

"Not now, Madge."

Blackstone darted past the pair, grabbing his coat in the waiting room. Three women, a child no older than five, and an older man turned their skulls to him, brains suspended in jelly. He couldn't see the expressions on their faces, but he could feel their fear. He felt sorry for scaring the kid especially, but he had to get the hell out of there.

"Martin, come back," Dr. Herbert cried as he dashed out the door.

Blackstone hopped into his car, peeling out, desperate to get as far away as possible from Madge and the terrifying thing living inside her.

# Chapter Ten

He breathed a sigh of relief when he came home to an empty house. Brian was in school and Andrea was out shopping. He hoped she'd be gone awhile. He needed to not see anyone for a while, just to give his senses time to recover.

What in blue hell was that thing inside Madge? Why was she the only one whose bones and organs disappeared, only to reveal that gut-churning foulness?

He dropped his coat on the living-room floor and sprinted up the stairs, just making it to the toilet. Vomit came out so hard and fast, it took his breath away. His eyes felt like they were going to pop out of their sockets. When he was done, he avoided looking in the mirror. He didn't think he could handle what he saw.

What if the thing inside Madge was in him as well?

He couldn't run from himself. Nor, knowing that, could he live with himself. There was only one way out of that situation and he was in no condition to entertain the thought of suicide.

Now what was he going to do? There was no way he was going back to Dr. Herbert's office. Even if he could be assured Madge wouldn't be within ten miles, he just couldn't face the doc after that episode.

He had to get these glasses off, pronto. He sat on the stairs, considering his options.

Holes.

It was too early for the tracks to be running, which meant he was most likely home. Hadn't he once worked in a drugstore? Yes, he had for a few years before retiring to the gambling life. He might be able to think of something.

Grabbing the phone book from atop the refrigerator, he dialed Holes's house.

"Yello," Holes answered.

"It's Marty. I need you to help me with something."

"Oh, hey Marty. Good timing. I was just about to step out and get the early racing forms. What's going on?"

"What kind of chemicals can eat away at industrial glue without doing any harm to the skin?"

There was a long pause. Blackstone could hear the radio news station playing in the background. There was a report about a decrease in oil production. Right now, he could give a frog's fat ass about oil. "What the heck are you talking about?" Holes said.

Blackstone had to keep from shouting. "Exactly what I just said."

"You accidentally glue something to your hand?"

"Yeah, something like that. You know of anything that'll work?"

"I can think of a couple of things."

Blackstone went rigid when he heard Andrea's car pull up to the garage door.

"Good. Grab what you can and meet me at the Rusty Nail." He had to get out before Andrea got home. He didn't want to see her again until he got the X-ray specs off. That he was pinning his hopes on Holes was a sure sign of his desperation.

"I'll see if I—"

He hung up before Holes could finish, slipping out the back door, grateful he'd parked on the street and wasn't blocked in by Andrea's car. He heard her close the front door just as he popped from the side of the house. Right now, she was probably calling his name. She'd get worried when he didn't answer and she looked out the window, only to see his car gone when it had just been there moments earlier.

Blackstone could live with that. Better a little worry now than her having to deal with a husband who'd gone stark raving mad, all over a pair of crap gimmick glasses that seemed to have been put together by the devil himself.

* * * *

It was just the two of them and Mike the bartender in the Rusty Nail. It was too early for the lunch crowd. Even the hardcore alcoholics were home, sleeping last night's bender off. Blackstone had a beer. Holes ordered a 7UP. He put a brown paper bag on the bar.

"All right, Ray Charles, what's the rush?" Holes sipped his soda, sitting back on the stool.

Pointing to the glasses, Blackstone said, "I gotta get these off."

Holes sputtered, soda spilling from his mouth. "How did you glue glasses to your face?"

"I didn't do it on purpose. Look, just help me and I'll owe you one. Or more than one." If he only knew.

At least neither Holes nor Mike had that black ooze inside them. It was the only positive thing to happen today.

Holes opened the bag. "Okay, I can see you're a little edgy. I get that. I wouldn't want cheap kid glasses stuck to my face, either. First, I got nail-polish remover."

Blackstone slapped the bar. "What are you gonna do, paint my nails?"

"Settle down, Marty. This stuff takes off more than polish, and it won't burn your skin. Well, you might feel a bit of a sting."

Grabbing a cocktail napkin, he soaked it and dabbed at Blackstone's temple. His skin tingled, the astringent smell burning his nose hairs. He had to close his eyes to avoid looking at Holes's bones touching his face.

He let it set in for a bit, then tried to pull the glasses off. They didn't budge.

"On to what's behind door number two," Holes said, slathering cooking oil on Blackstone's face. Some got under the glasses and in his eye, mercifully making everything blurry for a few minutes. "This one's my long shot, but it can't hurt to try. Oil is usually good at loosening glue, though maybe not the kind you got. How did this happen again?"

"If you get these off, I'll tell you."

They waited five minutes, Blackstone finishing his beer and ordering another. It was helping his hangover. Mike asked them what they were doing. "Experimenting," Holes said. The bartender left it at that. All that mattered was that they behaved themselves and paid for their drinks.

The oil didn't work. Neither did the bottle of glue remover he'd picked up from the hardware store. They each tried pulling the glasses off, sending sparks of pain across Blackstone's face.

"Jesus Christmas, it's like they're a part of you. You try seeing a doctor?"

He wasn't going to tell him what happened earlier, though Madge was surely spreading the word around at this moment. Fucking blackhearted nosy body.

"Maybe I *will* go to the emergency room like Andrea said."

Holes patted his arm. "Listen to her. She was always the brains in the family."

Blackstone pushed away from the bar. "Well, thanks for trying."

Holes was asking him about getting paid back for the things he bought when Blackstone walked out of the Rusty Nail and into the cold.

What he saw next brought him to his knees, screaming like a man who'd elected to forego anesthesia for his open-heart surgery.

# Chapter Eleven

Bodies brimming with brimstone were everywhere! They walked along the sidewalks, crossed streets, passed by in cars, sat in stores and offices. The sight of so many of them set something loose in Blackstone's brain. Even though they were all going about their business and paying him no mind, he felt that sooner rather than later, they'd turn on him because he could *see*. In an instant, he saw them for what they really were. And they would sense that, anger stoking the flames behind their crimson eyes as they set about making sure Blackstone could never, ever reveal their secrets.

He didn't do himself any favors by shrieking, his gibbering drawing the attention of everyone around him. Not all of them were filled with the boiling sludge, but there were enough to freeze his blood.

Holes burst from the bar, kneeling beside him.

"Whoa, what happened, Marty? You get hurt or something?"

Blackstone flinched when Holes went to touch him. "Lay off me, Holes!"

"Hey, I'm only trying to help you."

He stumbled to his feet, a dozen pairs of red eyes peering back at him. Could they see inside him too? Leaning against the wall, he scrunched his eyes closed.

Only this time, it didn't change a thing, because now he could see right through his eyelids.

"I—I can't make it stop," he stammered, backing away from Holes.

He heard his friend talking to the bartender, who had come outside as well, alarmed by the commotion. "Mike, how much did he have to drink before I got here?"

"He only had the two beers."

*I have to get out of here*, Blackstone thought, running from the Rusty Nail, weaving in and out of the skeletons and black souls out and about during the lunch rush.

Holes shouted something after him but he ignored him.

Black souls!

Yes. What he was seeing was their souls. Or their essence or whatever you'd want to call it. He never went for all that religious mumbo jumbo, but maybe they were right. It made a kind of insane sense. He'd always suspected Madge's prim propriety was a cover for something deep and dark. Seeing her soul for what it really was confirmed it.

There were so many people just like her, filled with vile muck, most pretending to be something they weren't…or maybe could never be.

He turned off Main Street, circling around residential roads, refusing to slow down, his breath coming in jagged gasps. His car was parked, of all places, by the real-estate office. Stacy Michaels's naked beauty being stripped away had started all of this. The last thing he wanted to do was look inside again, maybe seeing deeper into Stacy than anyone should.

Just don't turn your head in that direction, he said to himself, jogging around the block and coming back out on Main, two blocks back from the car. Skeletons and tainted souls were everywhere, carrying on with their day. None of them paid him any mind as he got into his car.

Gunning the engine, he thought of Brian's friend, Noel. He was the one who had bought the X-ray specs. Two pairs, in fact. The one pair was currently stuck to Blackstone's face, altering his vision, shattering his mind.

What about the kid? He'd kept his pair. And he hadn't been going to school.

Dammit, was the same thing happening to him?

He drove to Noel's house, unsure of what he was going to say when the kid's mother answered the door. All he knew at that moment was that he needed to see him. Whether it was to share in his misery or save him from a similar fate was up for debate.

\* \* \* \*

To his relief, Noel answered the door. Or at least what sounded like Noel. The bag of bones and pulsating heart could have been anyone.

"Oh, hi Mr. Blackstone."

He'd taken several deep breaths before leaving the car. The last thing he wanted to do was look and sound as frantic and out of control as he felt. He fumbled for words, unable to tell if Noel was wearing his X-ray specs or not.

"I—uh—heard you were sick," he finally said.

"The doctor says I have strep throat. I'll get my mom."

Before Blackstone could say anything, Noel walked away, shouting for his mother. It only made sense. Adults didn't come to houses to visit children. The last thing he wanted to do was talk to the woman, but it was unavoidable. He thought her name was Becky. They hadn't spoken much besides quick pleasantries in passing or when the boys were dropped off. Blackstone usually did his best to avoid her and her husband Hank. In the parlance of his mother, the couple wasn't his cup of tea. In his estimation, they were undercover hippies who he'd heard hosted key parties several times a year. He wouldn't be surprised if they smoked dope. He didn't have time for weed-smoking, granola-eating pansies. While he'd served in 'Nam, Hank was dodging the draft, protesting the war.

Nope, not his cup of tea at all.

"Mr. Blackstone's at the door," he heard the boy holler.

"Let him inside. It's freezing out. And get back on the couch."

The skeleton boy returned, opening the door wider. "My mother says to come in."

"I kinda got that. But I—"

Noel traipsed away before he could finish, the boy's image growing fuzzy for a moment before turning into the living room. Blackstone felt sparks of pain ripple across his chest. He shut his eyes for a moment, catching his breath, seeing through the floor into the basement. The vision startled him, his brain thinking he was floating on air for a moment and about to plummet.

Quickly recovering, he called out to the boy, "How do you like those X-ray glasses?"

His reply was barely audible over the TV. A rerun of *I Love Lucy* was on, part of the channel 5 morning schedule.

"Oh, that? I threw it away. It hurt my eyes."

Blackstone sagged with relief, but in a bizarre way was also upset. For it meant he alone was suffering in this hell. It wasn't right, hoping a child would endure the same torture. Nothing felt right anymore. Nothing.

"Hi, Martin. What brings you all the way to this end of the block?" Becky asked, emerging from the kitchen.

No!

The demonic soul walked steadily toward him. Blackstone's mouth went dry. He turned away just so he didn't have to see her hideous soul, catching a glimpse of himself in the mirror hanging on the wall next to him. He saw his own skeleton, brain sloshing slightly with the twisting of his head.

"Gah!"

"What is it?" she said, her usual casual Earth Mother voice tight with alarm. "Is it another of those silverfish? They've been all over the house lately."

He tore his gaze away from himself, settling his cursed eyes on the beast within the woman. The terror he felt was unlike any he'd ever experienced before. The darkness within Noel's mother was deeper than the pitch of deepest space, ten shades darker than hot tar, those hideous blood-red eyes boring into him. It felt as if he were being stabbed in the chest by those eyes!

"I—I." He couldn't form a coherent thought, so great was the unhinging of his mind. He wanted to run like hell, but his legs were cast in stone.

"Martin, you don't look well. Are you all right?"

She reached a hand out to him. He swatted her away, smacking her forearm as hard as he could.

"What the hell's the matter with you? You just hit me."

No, he thought, what the hell's the matter with *you*? How could someone's soul turn that putrid? What had she done in her past? Or worse yet, what had she been up to now?

Her hand reared back, prepared to deliver a blow across his face.

He couldn't let her touch him. Was the vile porridge within her contagious? There was no way to know. All he had to know was that she mustn't lay a hand on him.

Blackstone was just able to make out the outline of something in her other hand. It looked like a fondue pot. Before she could slap him, he grabbed the fondue pot, wresting it from her grip.

"What do you think you're doing?" she sputtered.

There was no time to think. Unadulterated panic had taken control. He swung the pot as hard as he could at the side of her head. It hit with a jolting crack. She didn't even make a sound. One second she was standing, the next she was on the floor. He could see the crack in her skull, the black ooze leaking onto the floor.

He jumped back, terrified of it touching his shoes.

"Mom?" Noel emerged from the living room. Lucy was in the next room talking to Ethel about throwing a surprise party for Ricky.

The small skeleton stepped into the hallway, looked up at Blackstone, then down at his mortally wounded mother.

"Mom!"

Blackstone tried to stop himself, but it was too late. The boy's cry of alarm set his arm in motion again. The fondue pot crashed into Noel's face. He heard the boy's nose snap, saw his cheekbones splinter.

Noel fell back several feet, landing in a heap amid a pile of shoes and boots by the front door.

"Oh sweet Christ! What have I done?"

The fondue pot clanked on the floor.

Blackstone swallowed back a tidal rush of bile. He ran from the house, having to step over Noel and push his body aside with the door. He never looked back.

# Chapter Twelve

*I just killed a kid.*

The five words circled round and round his brain as he sat in the car by the reservoir. There wasn't another person in sight. Snow had started to fall, enveloping the surrounding hill in complete silence.

It might have been peaceful if his thoughts weren't as loud as two freight trains colliding. Somewhere during his mad drive away from Noel's house, he'd shit himself raw. Sitting in his own reeking filth, he tried—unsuccessfully—to settle down. It was no use. Since he'd brained Becky and Noel, the X-ray specs felt as if they had melted partially into the flesh of his face. Touching them with trembling fingers, he didn't feel as much plastic as he had before. He was absorbing the glasses, slowly but surely.

A lone flying skeleton swooped overhead, most likely seeking shelter before the storm.

I didn't just kill a kid…I killed my son's best friend. Why?

Oddly, he felt no remorse for taking his mother's life. Pure evil bubbled within that woman. He didn't know or care how it got there. It was in her, at least until he gave it an opening to pour out, hopefully back to the hell from whence it came.

But the boy.

He'd simply reacted to seeing his mother bleeding to death on the floor.

And Blackstone, in his uncontrollable fit of fear, had killed him too.

Or maybe he's still alive.

The flicker of a thought made him sit up straighter, the mess in his pants stinging, fecal acid birthing nasty sores.

Noel hadn't been bleeding. Yes, his nose and part of his face were broken, but that shouldn't be fatal.

There was a very good chance he wasn't dead. His father should be home soon. He'd take care of him.

Blackstone moaned, eyes shut but able to see through the roof of the car.

He was still a murderer. No one would believe what he saw. Hell, he couldn't even get the glasses off to let the authorities see for themselves.

And even if he could, the blackness was surely gone by now, like spilled ink from a glass bottle.

If Noel was alive, he'd tell everyone who had killed his mother. Odds are, at this very moment, he was a wanted man, the local police putting out an APB for his arrest.

What the hell do I do?

Blackstone snickered.

Hell.

That was an appropriate word.

It was as if the glasses were giving him an insider's view of hell on earth.

"Maybe I should just claw my eyes out," he said, exhausted but nerves tingling.

He tried to slip a finger under the glasses to rub his eye. There wasn't even a sliver of space between the plastic and his skin anymore. Shit, if he stared crying, the tears would just collect until it would be like wearing a pair of full fish bowls.

And Lord knows, he wanted to cry. The last time he'd shed a tear was at his mother's funeral, right when they lowered her casket into the cold ground. He'd allowed himself a good minute to let the tears flow, Andrea sobbing beside him, rubbing his arm.

If he started now, they'd go on for much more than a minute.

Realistically, he should turn himself in. If he gave himself over to the authorities, told the whole truth no matter how bizarre and left himself to the mercy of professionals, he might be let off with no jail time. They would have to see how the X-ray specs had become a part of him. Maybe they could take them off with surgery. Let the military or scientists study the damn things. There was a good chance they'd raid the Honor & Smith Co. and arrest the owners as accessories to murder.

At this point, Blackstone didn't care if it left his face permanently disfigured. All that mattered was that they were off and his normal, everyday vision returned.

Another thought flitted briefly through his mind, but it was somehow more horrible than everything else.

Maybe it wasn't the glasses at all. Maybe, just maybe, he'd lost his fucking mind.

No! It was the damn glasses. He wasn't imagining that they wouldn't come off. He had witnesses to that fact.

*But are they really making you see souls?* A tiny voice whispered in his ear.

Sighing deeply, he started the car.

Going to the cops was his only choice. He couldn't go on the run. If he kept seeing people's skeletons and souls, he'd go mad, or maybe even kill himself.

Things were going to get worse, if not for him, certainly for Andrea and Brian. They'd have to live with the fact that he'd killed a woman and maybe her son. The fact that Becky was not an innocent wouldn't change things.

Before he went to the police station, he had to see his family one last time, no matter how repulsed he might be at the sight of them turned inside out. He just wanted to hear their voices.

He should also have a few beers while he was at it. It might be a long time before he had another.

Pulling the car onto Kendall Avenue, he drove with his eyes closed, seeing everything. Kendall was empty, but Main was crowded, people running to the markets and delis along the strip to get milk, eggs and butter before the snow really picked up.

"Enjoy your French toast," he said to the distant shapes, stopping at the light.

Leaning his elbow on the steering wheel so he could massage his head, he accidentally set off the horn. A couple walking in front of his car stopped, staring at him.

"Fuck!"

He mashed the accelerator, mowing them down, the Buick bouncing as it rolled over their bodies. A Ford truck nearly sideswiped him as he blew through the red light and swerved through the intersection. Horns blared. He thought he heard someone scream.

No matter. He had to do it.

The couple of black souls now hopefully lying dead back there had been something else entirely. In the outline of their see-through bodies, he'd seen gray faces twisted in torture within the swirling black mist.

They were already dead inside, vessels for the unspeakable.

Driving too fast over the light coating of snow, he nearly wiped out several times, taking turns without tapping the brake. He couldn't breathe right. His stomach cramped so hard, it was difficult to sit straight.

Just get home, he told himself over and over. Just get home and say your good-byes.

# Chapter Thirteen

Pulling into his driveway, the car fishtailed, back end scraping against the elm tree in the front of the house. Andrea's car was nowhere to be seen. He looked at his watch, but only saw through it to the working components. He had no idea what time it was or where she could be. The sun was blocked out by the storm clouds.

"Whoa, you all right?" he heard his neighbor Ron's voice call out when he opened the door. Blackstone looked over to the man's porch, or where it should be. A black shape stood in the open doorway. "That snow is treacherous. You really did a number on your car."

Blackstone had always liked Ron. He was a vet, just like him, having served overseas toward the end of Vietnam when things really went south, before the U.S. decided to haul ass out of the hopeless situation. Ron was always quick to lend a hand, helping him do some concrete work last summer on the front steps.

When Blackstone saw Ron now, he also saw a pair of screaming faces—children's faces. More to the point: the faces of Vietnamese children.

"Go back inside, Ron," he said, averting his gaze, slipping and falling when he tried to scoot around his car to his front steps.

"You been drinking, Marty?"

"No. Just leave me alone."

Blackstone struggled to regain his footing. He looked over when he heard Ron's gate open.

"Dammit, Ron, I said to buzz off!"

"Here, just let me help you up and get you inside."

Ron didn't buy that he wasn't drunk. Blackstone cowered from the man, a weeping girl no older than five locking her eyes on his, lips curled back in agony.

"What did you do?" Blackstone said, cowering from the man's outstretched hand. In his arm was the contorted face of a boy who bore a strong resemblance to the girl, tears streaming down his cheeks.

Ron chuckled. "It's more like what did *you* do, Marty. You're gonna have to take your car to the body shop. I can help you pound that dent out, but it'll need a pro to make it look right."

Blackstone managed to get on his feet without his neighbor's help.

"You never talk about what went on there."

"Huh?"

"Now I see why."

"You're not making any sense. Wow, you really tied one on, didn't you?"

Ron went to touch Blackstone again. He lashed out with his keys between his knuckles, burying them in the man's Adam's apple.

Gurgling, Ron clasped his hands over his throat, staggering into the tree and slipping onto his ass. He tried to say something, but it came out as an indecipherable sputter.

"I'm sorry," Blackstone said, the snow pattering his face. "I didn't want to see that. I didn't. But—but—"

There was no sense trying to explain himself to the dying man. He couldn't leave him out here for anyone walking or driving by to discover. Quickly, he dragged him across the inch of snow to the side of the house. He couldn't see if he'd left a trail of blood. All he could see were the roots and dirt under the sidewalk.

The house was warm and smelled like cookies. Andrea must have made some for Brian for when he came home from school. It was a slap in Blackstone's face, this scent of ordinary, domestic bliss. Even if he didn't go to prison, he'd never be able to go back to the way things were. Not after this.

All he could do now was sit and wait for Andrea and Brian to come home. Then he'd drive straight to the second precinct.

Standing at the refrigerator, he chugged two beers, tossing the empties in the sink.

Blood.

I probably have blood on my hands, he thought. He'd felt Ron's hot blood splatter all over him when he punched the keys through his throat. Running upstairs, he undressed, chucking his clothes in the hamper, changed and scrubbed his hands and face as hard as he could, unable to tell if he was having any success.

He made the mistake of raising his head, his reflection glaring back at him from the mirror.

Blackstone screamed.

His skeleton had been replaced by the black oil, the vaporous faces of Becky, Ron, the two people on the road and Noel writhing across the contours of his own face.

The center of his chest felt as though it had been pierced by a spear. Bolts of pain shot down his left arm. Shuffling backward, his back collided with the towel rack, ripping it off the wall.

"No! No! No!"

He couldn't take his eyes off the souls swimming in his body. Every life he'd taken he now carried within him.

It was hard to breathe. He gulped for air like a fish on land.

A cold fist squeezed his heart.

For the first time all day, his vision began to darken, a small, tender mercy before he slipped away.

His last thought before his heart gave out completely was, "Does anyone ever make it out of hell?"

\* \* \* \*

The moment Andrea saw the blood in the snow and bashed-in rear of Martin's car, she ordered Brian to stay in the car.

"What's wrong, Mom?"

"I don't know. Just stay here until I come back and get you."

She had a hard time getting her house keys from her purse. Even when she did, she dropped them twice.

Swinging the door open so hard that it banged against the foyer wall, she shouted, "Martin! Martin, are you all right?"

The house was deathly silent.

Judging by the amount of blood in the snow, there had been a really bad accident. Did Martin hit someone? Had he hurt himself? Was he in an ambulance right now? Too many terrible scenarios raced through her head.

"Martin."

There were empty cans of Schaefer in the sink.

Oh Jesus, was he driving drunk? She kept telling him to stay out of the damn Buick after he'd had a few. He swore he drove better drunk than most people sober. Only an idiot could think like that.

Running upstairs, she stopped in the bathroom and gasped.

Her husband lay on the floor, eyes wide open and staring at the ceiling, his face frozen in a rictus of raw terror.

Crying and sobbing his name, she knelt beside him, knees digging into the cold tiles, feeling for a pulse in his neck, knowing she wouldn't find any.

"Is Dad dead?"

Brian's small voice startled her. She tried to shield Martin's body from her son, knowing it was impossible. He'd seen more than any ten-year-old boy ever should.

"I need you to go to your room and close the door. I'm going to call an ambulance." Her voice quivered, words getting stuck in her throat.

"Did he get dizzy and hurt himself?" Brian said, pointing. She followed his finger to the pair of cheap glasses on the floor. The doctor must have gotten them off. So why had he still been carrying them around?

Slipping them in her pocket, she closed the bathroom door and hugged Brian. He either thought his father was still alive or in shock. His skinny frame absorbed her desperate embrace.

"I don't know, honey. We'll get a doctor here right away. Promise me you'll stay in your room?"

He nodded.

Andrea rushed to the bedroom to call 911.

She didn't hear the glasses fall from their precarious perch on the edge of her pocket.

Nor did she see Brian slip the X-ray specs on.

# Money Back Guarantee

*For Ginger, one cool chick with mad skills*

# Chapter One

*Edensbury, New Hampshire*

Survivor's "Eye of the Tiger" played for the millionth time on the radio, a crisp spring breeze tickling the back of Rosemary Lanchester's neck while she sat at the kitchen table calculating her take from last night's haul. It had been a hell of an evening. Her best so far.

"Almost better than robbing banks," she said. "Except much safer."

She paused and considered changing the station. "Eye of the Tiger" normally irritated her, its constant presence on both AM and FM bands this side of water torture. But the radio was across the kitchen on the fridge, and at this moment she thought, *I do have the eye of the tiger.*

She couldn't help but think of the Virginia Slims slogan, "You've Come a Long Way, Baby." Sure it was borderline sexist, but it drove the point home. She felt a brief shudder when she thought about how things could have gone for her.

"And they said I couldn't be domesticated," she said with a chuckle.

Now she craved a cigarette. But that wasn't going to happen. She'd quit a year ago, and despite countless urges, she hadn't picked up a single Slim since.

Gavin's leaden footsteps bumbled about upstairs. He'd be down any minute now, ready for his Sunday grapefruit and coffee. Rosemary couldn't wait to show him.

"Little hobby, my ass."

"Huh?"

Her son, Dwight, waltzed into the kitchen as silent as a stalking panther, sleep crust in the corners of his eyes, hair standing on end as if he'd jammed his finger in an electrical socket…again.

"Oh, nothing. You want some cereal?"

He eyed the paperwork scattered atop the table.

"Can I eat Sugar Pops in the living room? *Scooby-Doo* is on."

She poured him a bowl, added the tiniest splash of milk (he refused to eat cereal once it got soggy), and brought it to the coffee table in the living room, along with a cinnamon Pop-Tart and a glass of orange juice. He jammed his spoon into the center of the Sugar Pops, shoveling it in as fast as he could, eyes already glazed over from the sugar high while he watched Shaggy steal Scooby's snacks.

Gavin lumbered down the stairs in his brown yard-work slacks, itchy sweater that was so stained she wondered why she even bothered to wash it anymore, and battered Hush Puppies. It could be a hundred degrees and he had to wear that sweater to work on the yard. She swore he suffered through heat exhaustion just to embarrass her.

"Morning, babe," he said, kissing her on the cheek. He followed her into the kitchen. She took the grapefruit out of the fridge, cut it in half, and cleared a spot for him to eat.

"What's all this?" he said, working at the grapefruit with a serrated spoon. A squirt of juice splattered on his sweater. The old rag just absorbed the splotch, melding it with the others.

Rosemary imagined the other blemishes chanting, "One of us," as they accepted it into the family of filth.

She poured them each a cup of coffee and sat next to him, unable to keep her smile reaching from ear to ear.

"Those, my dear, are my sales slips from last night's Tupperware party."

He shuffled through the orders between sips of coffee. "What's this number here?"

"That's my commission for each sale. You want to know how much it adds up to?"

Gavin grinned. "I have a feeling no matter what I say, you're going to tell me anyway."

"Sixty-seven dollars!"

"Whoa. Are you kidding me?"

"Nope. And that's even with me taking out the money I spent on the fondue and snacks for the ladies. How do you like that?"

He reached over and squeezed her hand. "I love it. Being sequestered in our bedroom all night was definitely worth it. Sounded like one hell of a hen party."

Rosemary rolled her eyes. "That hen party was the sound of business."

"I'm only kidding. I'm really proud of you. Maybe I should take up selling Tupperware and be my own boss."

She stood and ruffled his hair. "Stick to your computers. You don't have the connections to make it in the Tupperware biz."

"Did Mom really make sixty-seven dollars?" Dwight said, startling her again. He had his empty bowl in hand. *There must be a commercial on*, Rosemary thought.

"She sure did," Gavin said.

"Stay right there. I wanna show you something." Dwight turned tail and ran upstairs.

Rosemary leaned against the sink and saw her husband get grapefruit juice on some order sheets. "Hey, be careful."

He held up his hands. "Don't blame me. It's the damn grapefruit."

She gathered everything up and moved the pile to the counter. She'd finish her paperwork after breakfast.

Dwight returned carrying a comic book. Rosemary saw it was the new issue of *Spider-Man* he'd begged for at the stationery store last week. He opened the comic to a page near the back.

"Since you have a whole lot of money now, can we order this? I promise, if you buy it I'll do all the chores around the house for a month."

"Hmm, I've heard that before," Rosemary said, taking the comic.

"If we get it soon, I can bring it to Jimmy's pool."

Rosemary had to stifle a chuckle. At nine, Dwight was a bundle of boundless enthusiasm. She knew that if she gave in to him, he would hold true to his promise about doing the chores ... for the first few days, at least.

"What is it this time?" Gavin said, slipping his plate into the dishwasher.

Rosemary looked at the full-page ad for a six-foot nuclear submarine. There were a ton of exclamation points touting all of its amazing features, including a working periscope, interior lighting, real control panel, and not just two but four torpedoes that a child could fire from his or her incredible nuclear submersible.

She showed the ad to her husband, who did not hold back his own laughter.

"Where are we supposed to keep a six-foot submarine?" he asked.

Dwight was quick on his feet. "The garage! We could put it over by the rakes and stuff."

"And you plan to do a lot of deepwater exploring?" Gavin said.

"Oh, yeah. And it fits two people, so Jimmy can come with me."

Rosemary read about the pride of ownership of a nuclear submarine, the most feared fighting ship in the high seas. Each sub went through rigorous field testing and would provide not just hours but entire days of fun and excitement.

"You know, I won't let your dad buy a microwave because I worry about radiation. This seems kind of dangerous."

Dwight sputtered, "But it's just *based* on a nuclear sub. They can't actually give nuclear stuff to kids."

"Oh, I see. That makes sense."

Gavin patted her ass when he walked by, heading toward the back door and a morning of mowing. "I'll let you guys decide this one. It would be kind of nice having our own submarine. You never know when it'll come in handy. I just hope it's better than those thousand army men that turned out to be thinner than paper and unable to stand up."

Dwight pointed at the ad with his slender finger. "Those army men were cheap. This is five dollars."

The sincerity in his conviction made Rosemary's heart ache.

She was feeling so good today, how could she say no? After all, she did have sixty-seven dollars that she hadn't had yesterday.

"Plus," Dwight added, "it has a money back guarantee. See, it's right at the bottom. Not that we'll need it. It'll be too awesome to give back."

Rosemary crouched down so they were eye level. "I'll tell you what—you go upstairs and get me an envelope and one stamp. I'll fill out the form and write a check and you can put it in the mail."

His eyes lit up and he draped his arms around her neck. His breath smelled sugary sweet.

"Thank you, Mommy! Thank you!"

Rosemary got her pocketbook out of the closet while he rooted around for an envelope. His excitement even had her heart beating a little faster.

Yep, she had the eye of the tiger today.

# Chapter Two

Tuesday nights were slotted for ceramics class with her friend Linda. Rosemary was currently working on a cute little Christmas tree with slots for colored cones of plastic that would look like lights once she turned on the twenty-five-watt bulb she'd install in the center of the hollow tree. It would look so nice on the radiator cover in the living room, the centerpiece of her Christmas village.

It was a little hard thinking of Christmas when the thermometer read ninety degrees. Rosemary had planned three more Tupperware parties between July and October. She'd earn enough extra money to make it the best Christmas the Lanchester abode had ever seen.

"You taking Linda or is it her turn to drive?" Gavin asked, helping to clean up after dinner.

"It's her turn. Why do you ask?"

"When I was coming home, I saw her stumbling out of the Dew Drop Inn. I don't think she was selling raffle tickets for the church relief fund."

Rosemary draped a dishtowel over her shoulder. Linda was having a rough time with her divorce. Vito wasn't making things easy. He was constantly popping by the house to buy their kids' affection, refusing to sign the final papers, and, when he'd had a few, threatening her over the phone. Or worst of all, that time he tried to break into the house at one in the morning. As far as Rosemary was concerned, Linda had every right to have a few at the Dew Drop Inn.

However, not at the expense of driving them into a tree. She grabbed Gavin and kissed him.

"I love you, you know that? Thank you for always looking out for me and Dwight."

He pulled her in for another kiss, his hands massaging her back, fingers slipping under her bra strap. She stepped away before things got too hot and heavy with their son in the next room.

"It's what I'm paid to do," he joked. She swatted him on the ass with the dishtowel.

The bell rang.

"I'll get it," Dwight sang out from the living room.

"A little early for ceramics," Gavin said, looking at the clock on the oven.

"Mom, Dad, can you come here?"

They hurried to the front door, bolstered by the strange tone in Dwight's voice. A deliveryman stood on the porch holding a clipboard.

"I just need someone to sign for this," he said. His shirt was dark with sweat rings. Even his mustache had a few drops of perspiration nestled in the short hairs. Rosemary quickly took the proffered pen and scribbled her signature on the delivery confirmation.

"Thank you. I'll be back in a sec," the sweaty postman said.

He shuffled to his truck, slowly getting a handcart out from a compartment in the back, and strapped a tall box onto it. It seemed to take him forever to wheel it to the porch.

Rosemary dashed to the kitchen and poured a glass of cold water from the tap. By the time she returned to the foyer, the deliveryman was unstrapping the box.

"You look like you could use a drink," she said, offering the glass.

"Thank you. I ask and ask for one of the new trucks with AC but I keep drawing that old jalopy." He guzzled the water, sighing with relief, and gave the glass back to her. "You all have a good night."

Gavin and Dwight carefully laid the box on its side.

"Is it heavy?" Rosemary asked.

"Not at all," Dwight said.

"What the heck can it be?"

Gavin bent down to read the shipping label. "It's from AdventureCo in Tegan's Mill, South Carolina."

Dwight started jumping up and down, cheering as if his Little League team had just won the championship. "It's my sub! It's my sub!"

"Your sub?" Gavin said, getting his pocketknife out. The pocketknife had been a gift from his late father. He never went anywhere without it.

"Yeah. The nuclear submarine Mom ordered for me!"

Rosemary smacked her forehead with the palm of her hand. "Of course. It was so long ago, I forgot all about it."

"Well, I didn't," Dwight said, on his knees watching his father run the knife along the edge of the box, slicing through the thick brown packing tape.

"Give me a little room, bud. I don't want to accidentally cut you."

Gavin had to saw away at the tape in some spots, followed by much heaving and ho-ing as they reached into the box and extracted the contents. Bits of Styrofoam and straw littered the floor. Rosemary bristled, each tug spilling scads of crud, which meant more sweeping and vacuuming when all was said and done.

"Huh," Gavin said, eyeing the long, flat slab of gray-colored cardboard. Dwight scooped up a folded sheet of paper that had fallen out of the box.

"It says some assembly required," he said, little of his zeal lost at the cheap appearance of his nuclear submarine that was currently flatter than a flapjack and looked like it would be as sturdy as ... well, a cardboard sub.

"I'm assuming I won't be needing a screwdriver or hammer," Gavin said, scratching the back of his neck.

Rosemary held her tongue. There was no sense denigrating the cheap piece of crap. Not when her son was so excited about it.

"Do you need my help?" she asked.

Dwight's brow was knit in deep concentration as he pored over the instructions. She looked over his shoulder and saw the poor artist's rendition of how the sub was supposed to, as it said at the top of the page, *Come to life with just a few simple steps!*

"Can you go back there and hold that part?" Dwight said, pointing to where he needed her to go without looking up from the page.

"Aye, aye, Captain," she replied, ruffling his hair.

"And Dad, you grab over there."

"Yes, sir."

Rosemary hoped Dwight wouldn't be too disappointed once everything was put together. Better yet, she prayed his imagination would win out over corporate greed and hucksterism, reimagining this obvious piece of crap into the wonder sub he'd been waiting weeks to get.

"Okay, when I say pull, you each tug on your end. The middle will pop out and I'll fold down the supports. You got it?"

"Got it," Gavin said with a wink.

Dwight paused for a moment. Rosemary thought she could see his little heart beating faster than a hummingbird's wings through his Incredible Hulk T-shirt.

"Ready. Set. Pull!"

She and Gavin gave a slight tug, afraid of ripping the thing in two. When nothing happened, they pulled harder. The sides of the sub began to bulge outward.

"Keep going," Dwight said, eyes wide, licking his lips. "You're almost there."

Rosemary was pulling so hard now, she almost lost her grip.

"This is harder than I thought," Gavin said. His tongue poked out of the side of his mouth, the way it always did when he struggled with something.

"But it's working," Rosemary said. Amazingly, it was taking the shape of a submarine. Her shoulder cracked, and then the top of the sub made a loud *pop* as it unfolded into place.

"Hold it just like that," Dwight said.

He stood over the sub, opened a square hatch at the top, and dipped his head inside. Pretty soon, he was in it up to his chest. She heard the scrape of cardboard being dragged and snapped into position.

When he emerged from the bowels of his tiny five-dollar submersible, beaming with pride, he announced, "You can let go now. She's all set."

Dwight looked it over from stem to stern. He breathed out a long "Wooooow."

Rosemary thanked God Dwight wasn't in tears. Gavin shook his head, but put on a happy face for their son.

"Looks like someone's ready to hunt some Russians," Gavin said.

Eyes glued to the flimsy sub, Dwight said, "I can kill a commie for Mommy."

"What did you say?" Rosemary said.

"A couple of kids in school have shirts that say that," he said.

Rosemary sighed, but she couldn't complain. She was the one who wanted him to go to public school where there was no dress code and kids could establish their own identities. Gavin had been a good Catholic schoolboy who'd wanted his son to follow in his footsteps. Except that Rosemary knew Gavin and his buddies when they went to St. Michael's. Every one of them was a devil in a blazer and clip-on tie. No way was she putting Dwight through that.

"Hey, someone has to. They don't call them the Red Menace for nothing," Gavin joked, doing his best to lighten her mood. He bent down to inspect the sub, reading the paper instructions. "Says it's supposed to be six feet long. I think they forgot to ship half of it."

Dwight crawled into the hatch, oblivious to his father's slight. "It's got a panel with all kinds of gauges and monitors," he said, his voice muffled in the cardboard box.

Rosemary put her arm around Gavin's waist. "Don't complain. If it was any bigger, we wouldn't have any place to put it without tripping over it ten times a day." Then she whispered, "And he loves it. God, to be nine again."

"Tell me about it. I remember spending entire summers playing with bottle caps I found in the street."

"Raise the periscope!" Dwight said.

Rosemary covered her mouth, laughing, when she saw the tube that looked just like an empty roll of paper towels poke out from the top of the sub.

"Dive! Dive! Dive!"

"I think he's forgotten we're here," Gavin said.

"Well, do you want to finish what you started back in the kitchen? Looks like we'll have at least fifteen minutes to ourselves."

Gavin's eyes lit up just the way Dwight's had when they pulled the sub out of the box. He knocked on the side of the sub.

"You okay in there, bud?"

Dwight responded with orders given to an imaginary officer.

Rosemary grabbed his hand and led him up the stairs. Their clothes were off before they crossed the bedroom threshold.

It wasn't until almost an hour later that they realized Dwight was still in the sub. They could hear him shouting orders to launch the torpedoes. Rosemary rested her head on Gavin's sweaty chest, her hand on his hardening cock.

"You have another in you?"

"Remind me to buy Dwight anything he asks for in those comic books," he said, pulling her on top of him so she straddled his face.

# Chapter Three

Rosemary got the frantic call from Edith Yancy just as she was struggling down the stairs with the old vacuum cleaner she'd inherited from her mother. It weighed more than Dwight and was louder than a pack of lions. She almost dropped it on her foot in her haste to answer the phone.

"The boys are okay, but I think you should come over," Edith said. She sounded like she was having a hard time catching her breath.

Rosemary went on instant high alert. "What happened?"

"They were in the pool…and"—Edith gasped—"well, I think it's just better if you were here."

"Is Dwight all right?"

"Yes."

*Oh, thank you, Jesus*, Rosemary thought, swallowing her heart back down her throat.

"And Jimmy?"

"Both boys are fine. Wet and a little shook up, but fine."

"I'll be right there."

Rosemary dashed out of the house, forgetting to close the back door. She ran across the street to Edith's. The front door opened before she could even knock. Edith stood there in her soaking wet clothes.

A single thought blazed across Rosemary's brain.

*She had to dive into the pool to save them!*

Edith's normally feathered bottle-blond hair was plastered to her skull, revealing dark roots.

"They're in the kitchen," Edith said.

"Are you all right?"

She gave a slow nod. "I really need to change. I'll be back down in a few."

Rosemary had to compose herself. She didn't want to barge in on the boys, buzzing with frantic energy. That would just upset them. She bit her lip, took a breath, and pushed through the swinging saloon doors.

Dwight and Jimmy sat at the kitchen table, towels over their shoulders, drinking from boxes of fruit punch. When Dwight saw her, his eyes were glassy with tears.

"It's ruined," he said.

She crouched down and smoothed the wet hair from his forehead. He really needed a haircut, but he kept insisting he wanted to grow it long, just like Jimmy, who looked like Shaun Cassidy's love child.

"Tell me what happened," she said, swallowing back the torrent of questions bubbling at the back of her tongue.

*Just keep calm. He's okay, and that's all that matters.*

"We really thought it would work," Jimmy said. He didn't look upset, or if he was, he hid it well.

Then it hit her.

"Dwight, did you put your submarine in the pool?"

He avoided eye contact. "Yes."

"You know it was made out of cardboard. Why would you do that?"

Now he looked up at her, twin streams of tears snaking down his tan cheeks.

"It seemed so strong, not like a box or anything. We wanted to try the periscope and see how the torpedoes would launch underwater." He finished with a sniffle. She noticed the puddle of water by his feet.

The torpedoes were black plastic cylinders that resembled lawn darts, only without a pointy end. Dwight had to shove them through an opening in the front of the sub. How did he not know that, at the very least, all of the water would run through that opening?

She had to remind herself that he was just a kid and kids did stupid things. She recalled her ill-fated attempt to be Mary Poppins in her aunt's backyard. She broke the umbrella *and* her ankle when she'd jumped off the shed.

"The whole thing collapsed around them," Edith said. She had a towel wrapped around her head and wore fresh tennis shorts and a flowered shirt. "I just happened to go out back to water my plants when I saw it sinking. I jumped in and pulled them out. Luckily, it broke apart real easy."

"I punched one of the walls right out," Jimmy said with a hint of pride.

Dwight leaned close to her and whispered, "I was scared."

She hugged him hard.

"You're all right now. Mrs. Yancy was right there, thank God."

He broke away from her embrace, rubbing his eyes with his knuckles, eyeing Jimmy, obviously ashamed for crying in front of his friend.

"I'm sorry," he said. "The submarine got totally destroyed."

"It's still in the pool," Edith said. She handed Rosemary a cup of instant coffee. "That stuff is heavy as H-E-double hockey sticks. Fred can fish it out when he gets home."

"I'm so sorry, Edith. Dwight should have known better. And now your pool is ruined."

Her neighbor waved her off. "The pool is fine. It just has some litter in it for the moment. And they *both* should have known better."

Jimmy piped up. "I told Dwight it would sink."

Edith rolled her eyes. "That sure didn't stop you from hopping right in and going down with the ship...so to speak."

"You're a true lifesaver," Rosemary said. She'd always held Jimmy's mother at a distance because of the way Gavin, and any other red-blooded male on the block, glanced at her whenever she walked by. She couldn't blame them. Edith was a suburban Lynda Carter, only with blond hair. Gavin would never do more than window shop, but the threat Edith posed made it difficult for all of the women in the neighborhood to warm up to her.

That would have to change. She'd saved her son's life, for goodness sake.

"I'm just glad I walked outside when it happened."

Before she could stop herself, Rosemary had her arms around Edith. "I can't thank you enough. I can have Gavin fish the cardboard out of the pool."

Edith was stiff at first, but settled into the appreciative hug. "No need. Fred could stand to help out a little more around here."

After several more thank-yous, Rosemary took Dwight home, Jimmy asking if he could come over later to watch TV.

"Why don't you put on some dry clothes," she said as they walked inside. "I'll fix you up a snack."

Dwight didn't say a word. Fresh tears brimmed along his lower lids.

She knew her son. He wasn't upset that he'd nearly drowned. He was young. In his mind, he was invincible.

No, he was crestfallen that his amazing nuclear submarine was now fifty pounds of wet gunk. She could hear him sobbing upstairs. At first, she wanted to cry, not just with him, but for him.

The more she thought about it, the angrier she got. What kind of company would sell impressionable children a water toy made out of cardboard? Dwight couldn't be the only kid who thought to take his sub into a pool.

She cut up an apple and poured some potato chips into a bowl, her jaw aching as she ground her wisdom teeth.

Didn't the ad say there was a money back guarantee?

Oh, she wanted her five dollars back.

Dwight came down, eyes red and puffy, biting his lower lip as he took the apple and chips into the yard.

AdventureCo was going to refund her money, *after* she gave them a good piece of her mind. She was about to ruin someone's day.

# Chapter Four

Gavin came home to a stressed-out wife and no dinner.

"Bad day?" he said, setting his briefcase on the counter. Rosemary had spent the better part of her day in the hot kitchen. Her sweaty hair was pulled back in a tight pony, a sleeveless shirt clinging to her. She'd wiped her makeup off hours ago and was chewing on the end of a pencil.

"We're going to have to have pizza night early this week," she said, running down the list of phone numbers she'd written on the pad and crossed off one by one. "I've been a little preoccupied."

He grabbed a cold beer from the refrigerator and leaned over her, rubbing her shoulder. "I can see. What have you been up to?"

She tilted her head up so he could kiss her. "Well, for starters, your son almost drowned today."

"What?" He nearly choked on Pabst foam.

Rosemary explained what had happened in Jimmy's pool, assuring him that Dwight was perfectly fine—at least physically.

"Where is he now?"

"Upstairs with Jimmy. I set the TV up from our room in his room. They're watching one of the *Planet of the Apes* movies, I think. I gave them enough soda and junk food to last them a week."

Gavin plopped into the seat opposite her, finishing off the beer and tossing the can in the garbage.

"Poor little bud. So what's all this?"

"I'm trying to find AdventureCo."

"Come again?"

"It's the company that makes the submarine. They're located in some little town I never heard of in South Carolina. At least that's what it says in the ad." She showed him the open copy of *Spider-Man*. "At first, I wanted to call them to ream them out. I figured since they offered your money back, they'd have a hotline to handle complaints."

Gavin got another beer, along with one for her, popping the tops and keeping the rings on his finger. "I'll bet there's no such number for the simple fact that everyone and their Aunt Ida would call to get their money back."

Rosemary tapped the side of her nose. "I've called information, the Better Business Bureau, the chamber of commerce in Tegan's Mill. I even called Marvel Comics to see if I could speak with someone in the advertising department."

"Wait, what's Tegan's Mill?"

"That little nothing town in South Carolina. I went to the library and got a map." She unfolded the map and jabbed a finger in the center of South Carolina. "At least the town is real. Now, if AdventureCo is actually there is another story. So far, it's not looking so good." She took a deep sip from the can. The cold beer was a welcome relief. Her guts had been burning all day, getting madder and madder as she struggled to find the shill company.

"Maybe you should let it go. The boys are okay. That's all that really matters."

"Yes, but it's just—"

"The principle. I'm very much aware of my wife's compulsion to set the record straight," Gavin interjected. "Look, you and I both know these companies are nothing but scam artists. They know it too, which is why they make it so hard to find them. Odds are if you do locate anything even remotely associated with this AdventureCo, it'll just be a little PO box with nary a human to yell at in sight."

Rosemary sighed, the tension that had kept her rigid as a steel pole all day easing just a bit. "I know you're right. But I can't let this go. You, Edith,, Fred and I could all be planning funerals tonight. We came that close."

Gavin got up, kissed the top of her head, and took the pencil from her hand. "All the more reason to be thankful and appreciate the fact that Dwight and Jimmy are at this moment gorging on sugar and salt and reveling in ape madness."

She stole a glance at the phone on the wall. There were a couple of other numbers she wanted to call. Gavin shifted and blocked her view. "So, instead of calling some rednecks in Bumbfuck County, order us up a couple of pies and let's eat and drink a bad day away. Work wasn't much of a picnic either. Come on, let's blow off some steam and get buzzed on a school night."

He nudged her with his elbow, eyebrows jumping up and down with that goofy smile that got her every time.

"Fine. For now. I still want my money back."

Chuckling, Gavin said, "I know you do. You're a dog with a bone. That's one of the things I love most about you. Well, that and your smoking-hot body, of course."

Naturally, Jimmy stayed for pizza—extra cheese with pepperoni—and before they knew it, all of the Pabst was gone and Rosemary was relaxed for the first time all day. Just in time to slip into bed.

Gavin came out of the bathroom, toothpaste in the corners of his mouth. "I think that Irish coffee was a bridge too far." He collapsed on his side of the bed, making Rosemary bounce and nearly pitch over the side. She giggled, hitting him with a pillow.

"You should call in sick tomorrow."

"Can't. I have a meeting with Bob and Dennis first thing in the morning. Should be stellar."

"I wish I could be a fly on the wall. Well, good night, honey. Thank you for taking the stick out of my butt."

He gave her a lingering kiss, his breath tasting of beer and toothpaste.

"It wasn't me. All the credit goes to the Pabst Brewing Company. And I'll bet you can call them any time you want."

Rosemary rolled onto her side, Gavin onto his, resting cheek to cheek. Sleep came hard and fast.

She dreamed she was back in school—fifth grade in St. Augustus Elementary School, to be exact. She was about to be called on by Mrs. Doyle to solve a fraction equation on the board when the fire alarm started ringing. She breathed a sigh of relief. She had no idea what the question even meant, much less how to get the answer. Fractions were a completely alien language to her. Mrs. Doyle had a habit of throwing chalk-encrusted erasers at students when they scribbled wrong answers. It didn't hurt, but it was humiliating.

"Nobody moves until Rosemary solves the equation," Mrs. Doyle said with a smug look on her spinster face.

"But the fire drill," William Fogerty said. He was a hall monitor and all around rules stickler. Everyone hated him, although at this moment, Rosemary was in love with the guy.

"What about it?"

"Don't we have to leave? There could be a fire."

"Anyone who gets up gets a month of Saturday detention." No one dared move a muscle, all eyes on Rosemary. "Well, princess, we're waiting. You wouldn't want us all to burn to death just because you're afraid of a little fraction, would you?"

Rosemary swallowed hard, knees knocking as she pushed her chair back from her desk with a loud *scriiiich!*

The fire bell rang incessantly. The shrill clanging pierced her eardrums as smoothly as a scalpel. She clamped her hands over her ears, drowning out the clamoring of the bell and, most of all, Mrs. Doyle's harsh invectives. She saw the old woman's wrinkled mouth move but couldn't hear a thing.

"You gonna get that?" Gavin said, nudging her.

"Whu?"

"The phone." The octave of his voice was at hangover depth.

Rosemary opened an eye and saw it was just after one in the morning. She fumbled for the phone, her brain trying desperately to wipe away the grade-school nightmare. A phone call this late could only be bad news.

She grabbed the received and cleared her throat. "Hello."

There was silence, but she thought she heard something humming in the background.

"Hello? Who's calling?"

"Fuck you, whore."

The man's voice was rough, scratchy, as if he'd gargled a handful of thumbtacks before dialing.

In her sleepy state, she wasn't sure she'd heard correctly.

*Why would someone call me a whore?*

"Excuse me, what did you say?"

The line went dead, the steady hum of the disconnect hurting her ear, just like the fire alarm in her dream.

"Who was it?" Gavin mumbled.

She had trouble getting the handset back onto the cradle. "Just a prank caller. Go back to sleep." She nestled the side of her face into the pillow, whispered, "Asshole," to the phone, and drifted off.

# Chapter Five

Rosemary and Gavin nursed hangovers and Dwight mercifully slept in. Gavin ate half a slice of toast before taking his coffee to go, hoping fresh air from the car ride would make him feel human before his meeting.

Rosemary drank two glasses of water from the tap and went outside, soaking up the morning sun before it got too hot. She sat in a lawn chair, dozing, when Dwight woke her up.

"Do we have any waffles?"

She yawned, stretched, and cupped his face in her hand. "We always have waffles. How many you want?"

"Two. With butter and syrup."

She grunted getting out of the chair. "Coming right up."

What almost came up was last night's pizza but she forced it down and by noon, she was back to normal. Dwight moped around the house. There was plenty of stuff to do around the place, so she drafted him into service. Asking him to help her move a few boxes in the garage was a mistake. When he saw the cleared spot where his submarine had been, he started to tear up again.

"I know I did something stupid, but can I get another submarine?"

Rosemary did her best to contain her shock. The damn thing had nearly killed him twenty-four hours ago and he already wanted another.

"I don't think so, honey. The place that makes them is a bad company. We're not going to buy anything from them again."

"But if they gave you your money back, you could use it to buy a replacement. You wouldn't lose anything. You already spent the five dollars."

She pushed a box of books along the floor. "That's not the point."

"Am I being punished?"

"Because I'm not buying you another submarine?"

He nodded, lip quivering.

The truth was, she had toyed with the idea of punishing him for what he had done, but she'd been too grateful to have him home and unharmed to go through with it. Plus, she'd been obsessed with finding those AdventureCo bastards.

"No, you're not punished. But I'm also not getting you another sub."

He dropped the box by her feet. "I hate you!"

Before she could respond, he was out the open garage door, heading for Jimmy's house. She watched him ring the bell and, after a few seconds, go inside without once looking back.

"What the hell was that all about?"

Unlike a lot of kids his age, Dwight had never been big on tantrums or back talk. He'd only told her he hated her once before, when she grounded him for riding his bike where she'd told him not to go, a passing neighbor alerting her as to how far he'd strayed.

Rosemary picked up the box and shoved it onto a shelf. "Fucking cheap sub. Wish I never ordered it."

That only reignited the flame to find someone, anyone, at AdventureCo and let them have it. Any chance of having peace of mind was nil until she had her say. She wished they were rich enough to afford a lawyer who could track AdventureCo down with ease and sue the mother-loving crap out of them.

The only lawyer they knew was Gavin's second cousin, and he did tax law out in Kansas. That wasn't going to do her any good. And knowing Ken, he'd probably charge them the full going rate.

She'd set this morning aside to write out invitations to her next Tupperware party, with an afternoon trip to the post office. They'd have to wait. Grabbing her pad and pen, she picked up where she'd left off and dialed.

This time, she called the office for the mayor of Tegan's Mill. She had no idea who the mayor was, but she'd gotten the number from the chamber of commerce. The mayor should be made aware that he...or she...was home to a shifty company that preyed on the dreams of children, only to hurt them, literally and figuratively.

"Mayor Gillespie's office," the young woman said, answering on the first ring. Rosemary sputtered at first, unprepared for such a rapid, and friendly, response.

"Um, hello, my name is Rosemary Lanchester. I'm, uh, not from Tegan's Mill. In fact, I live in New Hampshire."

Without hesitation, the woman said, "Not a problem. How can I help y'all?"

"I've been trying to find a company that says it's headquartered in Tegan's Mill. So far, I've gotten nowhere. I was hoping the mayor's office would know."

"I'm sure I can help. May I ask what this is in regards to?"

"Basically, I'd like to report them. They manufacture and sell dangerous toys to children. My son nearly drowned in one of their cheap products yesterday."

"Oh my! That's terrible. Is your son okay?"

"Yes, he's fine. He was shaken up, but now he's just upset that his toy is broken."

"Spoken like a true child. Bless his heart. How old is he?"

"He's nine."

Rosemary smiled, feeling some of the teakettle pressure bleed off. "I'm sorry, I didn't ask you your name."

"No, I'm sorry. I should have told you right off the bat. I'm Patty Runyon, Mayor Gillespie's secretary."

"It's so nice to hear a pleasant voice. I was like a dog chasing his tail yesterday, and no one was as nice as you."

"Why thank you. So, what's the name of this company? If they're operating out of our town, I'll either know them or be able to find them for you. And I'm sure Mayor Gillespie will have something to say to them as well."

Leaning against the kitchen counter, Rosemary couldn't help but smile. Everything she'd heard about southern hospitality was right. She made a mental note to send Patty some complimentary Tupperware to thank her for everything.

"Great. The company is called AdventureCo. They advertise in the back of comic books. They sell all kinds of junk, like those sea serpents that look like people, as well as X-ray glasses and the submarine that nearly cost my son his life."

There was a moment of silence. She thought she heard the scratching of pencil on paper. "Is AdventureCo all one word?"

"Yes."

"Hmm. Doesn't ring a bell. You said they sold your son a submarine?"

"It was just a long piece of cardboard with some paint. My son, thinking it was the real thing, took it into the pool with his friend."

"That's not good at all. I'll look into this for you and tell the mayor. What number can I call you back at, dear?"

Rosemary gave her number, thanking Patty again for being so nice and helpful.

She spent the rest of the morning waiting by the phone, drinking cup after cup of Sanka while nibbling on Stella Doro cookies. At noon, she called Edith and asked how the boys were doing. Despite the heat, the pool was off limits today. Edith's house had central air, so they were happy up in Jimmy's room reading comics and playing with his G.I. Joe figures. She was just about to make them grilled cheese sandwiches.

Thanking Edith again for saving Dwight, Rosemary turned on the tabletop fan and tried to read to take her mind off things.

"A watched phone never rings," she said, finding where she'd left off in Sidney Sheldon's *Master of the Game*. The four-hundred-page hardcover felt heavier than usual, the fan doing little to cool her off. It would be smart to read outside under the shade of the dogwood tree, but she didn't want to miss the call when it came.

She wasn't aware she had fallen asleep until the book thumped to the linoleum floor. She looked up at the clock. It was almost three.

"No more drinking on school nights," she said, massaging her temples. It felt as if the hangover was coming back, but that was impossible. She was just overheated.

After a quick trip upstairs to check the answering machine and finding she hadn't gone into a mini coma and slept through the call, she peed, washed her face and neck with cool water, and changed. During her nap in the kitchen chair, she'd soaked through her clothes. Her back ached from dozing in an odd position.

Not wanting to waste the entire day, she got some chicken out of the refrigerator and prepared breaded cutlets in the Shake 'n Bake bag. She also made a salad and cut up some potatoes so she could sauté them in butter later.

Food prep complete, she decided to tackle those invitations. She had over thirty to fill out. At least she could make a dent in them today.

She was writing one out to Mrs. Cranfield when the phone rang. She dropped her pen, scooted across the kitchen, and grabbed the phone.

"Hello."

"Is this Rosemary Lanchester?" the man said. He sounded old, his voice as brittle as an anthill.

"Yes, this is Rosemary."

"I'm Bob Gillespie. You spoke to my secretary earlier today."

"Oh, yes, thank you so much for calling me back."

"There is no AdventureCo in Tegan's Mill."

Rosemary's initial enthusiasm waned.

"Are you sure? That's the address they list in their ad."

"There is no AdventureCo in Tegan's Mill," he repeated, his voice flat and without emotion. It was like talking to a recording.

"Could they have been there in the recent past? I'm sure a place like that has to move around a lot, keep one step ahead of the complaints, or even the law. They have ads in all the comic books, so they have to be somewhere, spending good money to rip people off."

"They're not in my town, nor have they ever been in my town."

"I understand. I was just hoping—"

"Don't call my office again."

Rosemary stared at the phone as if she could look Mayor Gillespie in the eye and see if he was for real.

"Hello?"

The line was dead.

"Maybe I was wrong about southern hospitality."

She hung up and looked to her pad for the Better Business Bureau. This time, she called to file an official complaint, not just ask for information on AdventureCo. The person she spoke to took her information and complaint with cold efficiency. She was peppered with questions, which she answered, then thanked for taking the time to call before she was hung up on for the second time that day.

*No, make that three times*, she thought. She'd forgotten about the prank caller in the middle of the night.

Gavin came home, with Dwight not far behind, saving her from spiraling into her own angry thoughts. She made dinner and Dwight talked to her as if he hadn't yelled that he hated her and left in a huff earlier. That was fine by her. She needed some normalcy.

They ate and later watched *Happy Days* and *Laverne and Shirley* before Dwight had to head up to bed.

She never did tell Gavin about her calls or Dwight's outburst. No sense picking at the wound.

# Chapter Six

The box arrived a week later, addressed to Dwight. The postman didn't stay long enough for water this time. Rosemary looked at the return address.

AdventureCo, Tegan's Mill, South Carolina.

No street address. Not even a crummy PO box.

Dwight was across the street in Jimmy's pool. Using a pair of scissors, she opened the box and, after much struggling, extracted a new cardboard submarine. A sealed envelope was clipped to the instructions. She slid a nail under the flap and took out the handwritten note.

*"We're sorry to hear that your son experienced difficulties with his nuclear submarine. Please accept this replacement submarine as our way of showing our commitment to fun and quality."*

That was it. No signature. No acknowledgment that the *difficulties* had in fact been her son almost drowning in that cardboard joke.

"Commitment to fun and quality"? Were they fucking kidding?

If Rosemary's head wasn't screwed on tight, it would have spun off and rolled right out the door.

"I can't let Dwight see this."

There was no way in hell she would let her son play in this submarine or anything else from AdventureCo. She knew he'd never take it in the water again, but it was the damn principle. These scumbags didn't care that their product had nearly killed her son. This was just their lame way of saving some face. They most likely got wind of her complaint to the Better Business Bureau. So what was their solution? Send the same dangerous contraption to finish the job?

They didn't even refund her money, the very least they could have done, and what they vowed to do in their ad. Not that she held any credence in anything they put in print.

She went to the garage and rummaged around Gavin's battered toolbox until she found the box cutter. Easing the blade out with her thumb, she went back to the foyer and got to work slicing the sub and the box it came in into manageable rectangles. After arranging it into a small tower, she tied it all up with twine and dragged it outside, laying it next to the garbage cans on the side of the house.

Dwight returned wearing his flip-flops, a wet towel over his shoulder, just as she stepped into the front yard.

"Were you jogging?" he asked.

"Huh?"

"You look the way you do when you jog."

She wiped at her forehead, slathering salty sweat down her face and into her eyes. She'd been so focused on destroying the sub that she hadn't even noticed the heat.

"I was just busy doing some cleaning. You have fun at Jimmy's?"

"Yeah. He has to go with his mom to the allergist, but he said I can come over later, if that's okay with you."

As much as she wanted her son with her, their house was no match for central air and a pool.

"Okay, but only if Jimmy lets us repay him by taking you both to see *Superman III*."

Dwight's eyes lit up. "Really?"

She hugged him and kissed his chlorinated hair. "Really. We can catch the matinee at the Katonah tomorrow."

He squeezed her as hard as he could. "You're the best."

She watched him practically skip inside.

Would he say that if he knew what she'd just done to his new submarine? No matter. She had done the right thing.

Besides, she wanted to see *Superman III*, too. That Christopher Reeve wasn't bad to look at, especially in those tights.

\* \* \* \*

They went to the movies the next day, and because she was feeling guilty, she let Dwight buy anything he wanted at the concession counter. That meant she sprung for the large buttered popcorn, Junior Mints, Twizzlers, and some off-brand peanut butter cups. The boys tore into the snacks like starved wolverines. It didn't take any special mommy senses to see that she'd be consoling a son sick to his stomach all night long.

Just something else to feel guilty about.

And to make matters worse, the movie was terrible. Gavin had taken her to the drive-in to see the first two Superman movies and even though they were cheesy, she liked them all the same. This latest installment was an eye-rolling disaster. But Dwight and Jimmy loved it and in the end, that was all that mattered.

Plus, the air conditioning was set on arctic blast, which felt wonderful. It had been a sweltering summer. She didn't mind shivering midway through the movie.

"Can I be Superman for Halloween?" Dwight asked after they dropped Jimmy off at his house.

"Isn't it a little early to be thinking about Halloween?"

"Yeah, maybe, but the second they put out the costumes at Woolworth's, we have to get one."

When she opened the front door, the trapped heat in the closed-up house punched them in the face.

"You got it," she said, fanning herself as she dropped her keys on the little table in the foyer. By the time Halloween rolled around, Dwight would have changed his mind about what he wanted to be at least a dozen times.

"I'm going outside," Dwight said, heading for the yard. She heard the water turn on and the spritz of the sprinkler by the patio. She looked out the back window. Dwight stood over the sprinkler, getting soaked in his clothes. At least he'd had the good sense to take his sneakers off.

Rosemary was tempted to get in her bathing suit and join him. The varicose veins that had come along with her pregnancy nine years ago had only gotten worse. She rarely wore anything that revealed her legs, even though there were just a few starbursts of spider veins on her calves. She was even self-conscious about them in the privacy of her own yard.

But it looked so cool and inviting.

When she was a kid, she didn't know anyone who had a pool. A sprinkler or the occasional fire hydrant that was opened by the fire department were the only ways to cool off on hot days, other than taking a cold shower.

Dwight unscrewed the sprinkler so he could drink greedily from the hose, cold water splashing across his face as he lapped it up. There was no water on earth crisper and more thirst quenching than that from a summer hose.

"That's it, I'm going out there."

The phone rang just as she was about to leave the kitchen. She picked it up on the second ring, knowing it was probably some telemarketer who she'd give the brush off, though there was always a chance it was Gavin or her parents.

"Hello," she said, sounding more chipper than usual. She really wanted to get out there and join Dwight in the fun.

"You shouldn't have done that," the cold, flat voice said.

"What?"

"That wasn't very nice."

"Who is this?"

"It wasn't yours to destroy."

"Destroy?"

Rosemary's chest tightened. No. It couldn't be.

"Did you really think you could get away with it? It wasn't meant for you."

Her hand gripped the phone so hard, her knuckles cracked. "Look, I don't appreciate you calling me and speaking to me like this. Who do you think you are?"

"We take customer complaints very seriously." There was a pause where all she could hear was heavy breathing. "*Very* seriously."

"I know where you're calling from. Let me speak to a manager."

There was a low, filthy chuckle. "You thought you got away with it, didn't you? Poor mommy. You can't protect him forever."

She thought she was going to pass out, the sudden rush of blood to her head overwhelming.

"I'll…I'll call the police."

"You'll have enough on your hands. Right…about…now."

She leaped out of her skin when the door opened. She dropped the phone. It slapped against the wall, twisting on its coiled cord.

"What did you do?"

Dwight held one of the stacks of cardboard that had been his replacement submarine. He dripped all over the floor, his hair in his eyes.

Rosemary was stunned speechless.

"Why didn't you tell me they sent me another one? And why did you destroy it?"

"I…I did it to protect you, honey."

He threw the cardboard at her feet. "You did it because you're mean. You were happy when the first one was destroyed."

She reached out to him but he stepped back several paces, as if her touch were acid. "No, no, no, that's not it at all."

"You're a liar. You didn't tell me anything. That makes you a liar."

Rosemary didn't appreciate being called a liar, but the phone call and this sudden confrontation with her son had her on her heels. All of her mothering skills fled her in the moment. She was on the verge of tears, seeing the hurt in Dwight's eyes, hearing the accusations from his mouth.

"I never want to talk to you again," he said, bustling past her. He flicked her hand away when she went to touch his shoulder, to calm him down and try to somehow explain in a way he'd understand. It was probably a good thing he left, because her brain's inertia wouldn't have been able to come up with two coherent sentences in a row.

Dwight stomped up to his room and slammed the door. She heard the bedsprings creak as he threw himself onto the mattress.

She couldn't take her eyes off the tied-up pile of painted cardboard. If she could incinerate it with a glance, she would have reduced it to ash.

The tinny sound of laughter sent icy footsteps down her spine. She looked at the phone, spinning clockwise by her ankles. Reaching over to pick it up, she reluctantly put the receiver to her ear. The laughter stopped, as if whoever was on the other end could see her.

"Don't fuck with us. We mean it."

Her lips were moving, no sound coming out of her mouth, when the phone went dead. As if in a trance, she slowly hung up, pulling a chair out so she could sit staring at the cardboard.

What the hell had just happened?

She was scared and angry and sad that she'd hurt Dwight. It was all too much. Rosemary buried her face in her hands and cried.

A terrifying thought snapped her out of her crying jag.

The man on the phone had known exactly when Dwight was going to come into the house, upset with his discovery.

Which meant that man was outside, watching them. She got up so fast the chair skittered across the floor. She rushed from window to window, searching for any sign of a man nearby. After checking, she shut each set of blinds until the house was cocooned in darkness.

Just because she didn't see anyone didn't mean they weren't out there. Maybe he was sitting in that blue van across the street, the tinting on the windows so dark she'd need to be Superman to see through them.

As much as she wanted to run up to the van and peer inside, she couldn't bring herself to do it. She was too afraid to even touch the knob on the front door. Grabbing Gavin's softball bat from the closet, she hunkered down in a chair in the living room, senses on high alert.

But if he was in the van, how did he call her?

Was he in one of her neighbor's houses?

She shivered at the thought.

Dwight clomped about in his room, slamming things on the floor.

She checked the clock. Gavin wouldn't be home for another two hours.

It would be the longest two hours of her life.

# Chapter Seven

After a thorough search of not just their yards but every car parked on the street, Gavin returned drenched in sweat, his tie loosened, the top buttons of his shirt undone, stray chest hairs poking out from his undershirt.

"You see anything?" she asked, still clutching the bat. The moment Gavin had walked in the door, she'd told him everything in a frantic burst. At first he'd had to ask her to slow down and repeat herself, his mind trying to catch up with everything. After the second iteration, he'd told her to sit tight and lock the door while he went outside to look for the man.

"Nothing. Except for George walking his dog. Whoever it was must have taken off right after the call. Damn coward. Does Dwight know?"

She shook her head. "He's been in his room the whole time."

Gavin wiped the sweat from the back of his neck. "Well, that's one good thing."

"What do we do now?"

"I'm calling the cops. I'm not letting some psycho threaten my wife and lurk around my house. This is why I told you I should have a gun."

She didn't want to get into the old gun argument again. Not now.

He got a beer out of the refrigerator, thought better of it, and put it back. "If they come here for a statement, I don't want them thinking we were drunk and imagined the whole thing."

While he dialed 911, she hoped Dwight stayed upstairs a little longer. She didn't want him to overhear anything.

Gavin took charge, explaining everything to the police as calmly and succinctly as possible. Rosemary wasn't sure she could have done it even half as well. Her nerves were a jangled mess. Her husband had always been at his best when things were at their worst.

After five minutes, he thanked them and hung up. Then he went back and got that beer.

"Are they coming?"

"He said there's no need. If there are any more calls or if we spot someone around the house who shouldn't be here, we should call again and they'll send someone right away."

"Shouldn't they tap the phone or something so they can find him?"

Gavin smiled for the first time since getting home. "I'm pretty sure they don't think this rates a wiretap. Though I'd give anything to find where the call came from and wipe the floor with his face."

He wrapped a strong arm around her, rubbing her shoulder. "I'm so sorry you had to be the one to get the call."

"You have nothing to be sorry for."

Gavin tensed and said, "Hey, bud. Just in time to order Chinese."

Dwight eyed them suspiciously, but said nothing. Rosemary couldn't help but notice that he avoided her gaze.

"I'm not hungry," he said.

"Bud's not hungry? Call a priest. I think we have one of the signs of the apocalypse."

Gavin did his best to release the pressure in the room, working harder than a Catskill comedian on free appetizer night. Dwight was too upset to play along. He simply turned and walked back up to his room.

"Wow. He's pissed," Gavin said.

"I guess he has a right to be."

"Uh-uh. No way. Not after the way that asshole spoke to you. The last thing we want is our son playing with anything from that…what's it called?"

Just saying the name formed a cold fist in the pit of her stomach. "AdventureCo."

He put down the beer and hefted the bat.

"Well, if AdventureCo knows what's good for them, they'll have had their fun and are long gone, never to return. Because if I catch any of them around here, it's going to get ugly."

Rosemary shivered despite the cloying heat.

Things were already ugly.

* * * *

Despite Gavin being on watch, Rosemary barely slept. She wasn't sure what kept her up more—the hurt in Dwight's eyes over what she'd done or the terror she felt from yesterday's phone call. The sheets were a tangled mess. The overhead fan did little to cool her down. Her skin felt like it was on fire.

Gavin had called his boss last night, leaving a message that he wouldn't be in today. He stayed downstairs all night in the dark, waiting to see if the mystery man from AdventureCo returned. She'd heard him prowling about all night, but he'd been quiet the past hour or so. The sun was just peeking over the horizon, an orange glow emanating past the edges of the closed blinds.

There was no point trying to sleep. Rosemary got up and went to the bathroom. She'd make Gavin a lumberjack breakfast, complete with pancakes, eggs, sausage, and home fries. He'd earned it. She hoped a full belly would help him sleep during the light of day.

"Chow time for the sentry," she said as she walked into the living room. She expected to see Gavin passed out in his favorite chair or on the couch.

He wasn't in the living room. She went to the empty kitchen, then the garage. No Gavin.

Peering out through the blinds, she checked to see if he was making a pass around the house. When she was at the living room window, she noticed his bat propped up against an end table.

"Gavin?"

She went upstairs, wondering if he'd gone to check on Dwight. Her son lay sprawled out on the bed, mouth hanging open, a line of drool going from his cheek to his *Star Wars* pillowcase.

Even though it made no sense, she checked the attic.

Her husband was nowhere to be found.

Trying to steady her nerves, she went back downstairs and made pancakes. Maybe he went out to get the paper. Bond's Stationery Store was just six blocks away, and Gavin sometimes walked there when he was up early to get a paper, a cup of coffee, and the latest issue of *Popular Mechanics*. All manly stuff.

*That's where he is. Stop being a worry wart.*

The house was locked up tight. No one had broken in and kidnapped Gavin. Even if someone had tried, she was sure Gavin would have made enough noise to wake the dead.

After making a dozen pancakes and getting the home fries sizzling in the pan, she couldn't swallow her heart down her throat. Even if he'd gone to Bond's, he should be back by now.

What was she supposed to do now? If she panicked and called the cops and Gavin came back from wherever he'd gone, both he and the police would be pissed at her.

*But what if he doesn't come back?*

How long did you have to wait before someone was declared missing? Was it twenty-four or forty-eight hours? She couldn't remember. How long had Gavin technically been missing? Would it start from the moment she stopped hearing him move about downstairs, or now, when she realized he wasn't here?

Rosemary's head spun. She plopped into a chair, ignoring the home fries, smelling them start to burn. The smoke alarm went off. She fumbled to get the batteries out. Footsteps thumped down the stairs. Dwight shuffled in, rubbing his eyes.

"Are we on fire?"

She fought to keep her voice calm and steady. "No, it's just your mother burning breakfast."

He saw the pancakes and licked his lips. She set him up with two, coating them with butter and syrup. He dug in, talking to her as if yesterday had never happened.

*At least that's one thing off my mind*, she thought. But it had only been replaced by grave concern for her husband's whereabouts. Her son didn't ask where his father was because Gavin was usually at work by now.

"Is it really supposed to rain today?" Dwight asked through a mouthful of sweetened fluff.

"Um, that's what they said on the news last night."

"Oh man, that means no swimming. I hate rainy days in the summer. They're so boring."

She gave him a shaky smile. If only he knew how *not boring* today would be if his father didn't come back home.

He finished his pancakes and went into the living room to watch TV. Rosemary cleaned up after him, noticing the slight tremble in her hands.

"Gavin, where the hell are you?" she whispered to her reflection in the windowpane over the sink. "Please get back here and let me know you're all right."

She bit her lip to hold back tears. Dwight laughed at something on TV. Rosemary felt like screaming.

# Chapter Eight

"Can I go to Jimmy's and read comic books?"

"No!" Rosemary snapped. She'd been nervously sipping coffee, staring at the front door, waiting—no, pleading for it—to open.

"Why not?"

She saw the bundle of comics tucked under his arm. Outside, there was a light drizzle, the darkening skies portents for worse to come.

"Because I want you home today."

"Why?"

"Because I said so. And that's final."

Dwight looked as if he were about to protest, but the sharp glare he got from his mother stopped him cold. Instead, he snorted and marched back up the stairs.

"Guess I'm back on the shit list," she said. No matter. There was no way she was letting him out of her sight today. Since breakfast, she'd gone to his room to check on him at least ten times. All he did was act out scenes from *The Empire Strikes Back* with his figures, getting more and more irritated that she kept barging in on him. At one point, she went to his desk to look at the plastic tank that contained the Amazing Sea Serpents she'd bought for him at Woolworth's after much begging. The tiny wriggling balls of gray were disgusting. She kept waiting for them to die so she could toss the whole thing out. His room was starting to get a funky smell from them.

Normally, she would have flushed them, but after everything with her destroying his replacement sub, she let it be…for now. In a couple of days, she'd need a mask just to be able to stand in the room. It was amazing how Dwight didn't seem to notice the rotting funk.

Now it was almost noon and Gavin had been gone for six hours. It was time to call the police. She couldn't wait another second.

Just as her fingers touched the phone, it started to ring, the vibration traveling up her arm. She snatched it up.

"Gavin?"

A woman replied, "I'm calling to confirm a delivery."

"A what?"

Her doorbell rang.

"Thank you for your time," the woman said and hung up.

Rosemary dropped the phone and raced to the door. What if Gavin had gone out and gotten hurt? Maybe he'd been run over by a car? That could be the police at her door.

She threw the door wide open.

It wasn't the police.

It wasn't anyone.

Just a tall box standing erect like the monolith in that *2001: A Space Odyssey* movie.

She didn't have to look at the label to know what it was and where it was from.

Stepping around the box, she looked up and down the street for any sign of the person who could have left it there. The rain was beginning to pick up. The wet street was devoid of cars, other than the few familiar ones parked on either side.

How the hell could someone have rung the bell and vanished without a trace so quickly?

Breathing heavily, her hair drenched, she walked back to her porch, kicking the box over. The edge landed in a small puddle, splashing rainwater on her legs.

"You son of a bitch."

She brought her foot down on the box, hearing the satisfying crunch of the submarine inside breaking. She kicked and stomped it until her legs were sore, the box a mangled mess.

Slamming the door, she leaned against it, tears burning as they rolled down her cheeks. She would have to drag the box to the garbage so Dwight didn't find it...again.

Or would AdventureCo find a way to make sure he saw what she'd done?

She couldn't help feeling as if they were being watched, even in the house.

When the phone rang, her bowels turned to ice. Slowly, she made her way to the handset, bringing it close to her ear but not allowing it to touch her skin, as if it would bite.

"I told you not to do that, you dumb bitch."

She couldn't control her trembling. She was unable to speak. Snot poured from her nose as she silently wept.

"Now that makes two," the gravelly voiced man said.

Rosemary took a great breath and spat out, "Who the hell are you? I don't care what you told me. I'll destroy everything you send."

There was that chuckle again.

"You don't get it. Take a deep breath, sister, and listen to my words."

Rosemary had to hold the phone with both hands to keep from dropping it.

"Now...that...makes...two," he repeated.

"That's very good. You can count."

"Oh, but can you? Ta-ta."

She slammed the phone down with a primal scream. She had to compose herself and call the police. There was evidence right on the fucking porch.

Just as she slipped her finger into the round slot for nine, the man's words repeated themselves.

*Now...that...makes...two.*

The phone slipped from her fingers and she ran upstairs. "Dwight! Dwight!"

His room was empty. His Luke Skywalker figure stood on the floor, facing her, lightsaber extracted.

"Dwight?"

Just as she'd done earlier searching for Gavin, she went from top to bottom of the house, only this time weeping and crying out her son's name until her throat was raw.

"My baby. They took my baby."

She collapsed on the foyer floor, feeling as if every bone, every scrap of muscles and sinew had been sucked clean from her body.

When the phone rang this time, she had to crawl on her hands and knees to answer it. She felt drugged, wasted, soulless.

"Call the police and they die."

"What...have you done... with them?" she said through hitching breaths.

"Thank you for choosing AdventureCo, where imagination becomes reality. Have a wonderful day. Fucker."

# Chapter Nine

Rosemary lay curled in a ball, the phone by her head, the monotonous, shrill tone of the disconnection sounding miles away. She cried until her eyes were dry, until her stomach cramped and her chest hurt.

How was any of this possible? How could they have snatched Gavin and Dwight right out from under her without making a sound? It almost seemed supernatural.

She wrestled with herself about calling the police. It seemed as if AdventureCo could see and hear every move she made. They'd know the moment she dialed 911. And then what? Would they actually kill her son and husband?

Yes, she decided. Yes, they would.

These people were monsters, if they could even be called people.

Dragging herself into a standing position by gripping the front door knob, she opened it to see if they'd taken the box away, too. It was still there, soaked through from the rain. She dragged it inside, shutting the door with her foot.

The label didn't reveal any more than the name of the company and the town and state. A town where even the mayor refused to acknowledge that the company existed.

What the hell was AdventureCo? They weren't just a toy manufacturer, that was for sure. If anything, they had all the abilities and influence of a secret government agency.

But why would the government want to hurt and kidnap kids through the false front of a shitty novelty toy company?

Nothing was making any sense.

She stared at the label, fingers pushing through the wet cardboard.

There was really only one thing to do.

She had to go to Tegan's Mill, South Carolina, and find her family. It was a long shot, but it was all she had.

Fearing that her house was somehow bugged, she didn't bother packing anything. She simply grabbed her car keys and left. She had a very important stop to make. It was one she'd hoped to never revisit.

\* \* \* \*

"Am I hallucinating?"

Rosemary sighed and pushed her way through the steel door. "Trust me, this feels just as strange for me."

"I'd hug you but I'm afraid you'd knee me in the nuts."

She put her hands on her hips and stared at her brother. Five years older than her, he looked triple that, his hair gone mostly gray, unshaven, a bit of a paunch, his badge of honor from being a member of the six-pack-a-day club.

"Now why would I go and do that?" she said.

He scratched at the salt-and-pepper whiskers under his chin. "Because that's exactly what you did the last time I saw you."

"I was just a kid and if I recall correctly, you earned it."

He let out a laugh bordering on a guffaw. "I think you might be right. Big brothers are supposed to push their little sister's buttons. Come on over here."

As he held her tight, all she could fixate on was the smell of grease and cordite coming off his clothes and skin.

"So, what brings the black sheep back into the fold?" he asked, eyeballing her from head to toe. "You been a redhead for long?"

"Only since I left. Look, Rob, I need your help."

Her brother raised his hands in the air and staggered back, pantomiming someone at a faith healing show. "Lord, today must be thy day of judgment, for you have performed great and mighty miracles."

Rosemary cocked an eyebrow. "It's good to see you haven't changed a bit. Personal growth was never one of your strong suits."

He gave her a wink. "Maybe not, but when it comes to personal protection, I'm the master." He offered her a seat in the sparsely furnished shed, a battered chair he must have plucked from a dumpster. Taking one opposite her, their knees almost touching, he grew somber. "I know this has to be something serious to get you all the way the hell out here. You're my sister. Not seeing you for a decade doesn't change that. What can I do to help?"

Rosemary had to fight back tears. Her emotions were riding so high, she wouldn't be able to see the crest with a telescope. Seeing Rob now sent them to the stratosphere.

So much bad shit had gone down between them... but she had to admit, there had been good times, too. Despite their age difference, they'd been pretty much alike growing up. So much so that it frightened her to think back on it. He'd just taken his own path, and maybe it was time to forgive and forget. After all, it was his life choice that might get her family out of this jam.

"Somebody kidnapped my family," she said into her lap, biting her bottom lip hard.

"Come again? I didn't know you have a family."

When she looked up, she saw his incredulous face through a haze of tears. "I married Gavin after college. We had Dwight nine years ago."

Rob took her hands in his own calloused paws. "I'll be damned. I have a nephew named Dwight. I just never heard of a father and son being kidnapped. Usually it's one or the other."

She took a deep, tremulous breath. "This is going to sound insane, but I swear to you, it's all true."

His eyes locked on hers. "Tell me. I believe you."

It all came out, from ordering the submarine from AdventureCo after her Tupperware success to what had happened earlier in the day. To Rob's credit, he didn't once interrupt her, never questioned a single thing. His jaw just got tighter and tighter the more she talked.

When she was done, he sat back in his chair and wiped his brow with a bandana he had in his back pocket. The air in the shed was stifling. "You said Tegan's Mill, South Carolina?"

"Uh-huh. Except no one in that town has ever heard of the place."

He got up and offered his hand. "Come with me. You can settle down a bit while I make some calls. You okay with ladders?"

"I think I can handle it."

They went to the back of the shed where he pushed an old wood pallet aside, grabbed an iron ring in the floor, and pulled a hatch up. They descended to his underground bunker using the rungs positioned along the sheer steel wall.

"You've gone even deeper," Rosemary said, her voice echoing in the narrow tube.

"The commies keep making those nukes bigger, which means I have to get farther away. Shit, I'm so far down now, I don't even think I'd hear a bomb if it dropped on my head."

They finally came to a round chamber made of discarded metal. A series of tubular passageways branched out like the spokes on a wheel. Years ago, Rob had bought used yellow school buses, burying them deep and using them as the foundation for his growing fortress. He removed the seats, sealed up the windows, and filled them with all of the supplies he felt necessary to ride out a nuclear apocalypse. Everyone thought he was crazy. Cold War fever had driven him mad with paranoia. Their father had similarly gone off the deep end after the whole Bay of Pigs near-fiasco. He'd eventually left the family to go live in the woods somewhere in Canada. When they were kids, Rob blamed their mother for not supporting him and letting him leave. In hindsight it was ridiculous, but at the time, Rosemary sided with her brother. As they got older, they each took an interest in post-war survival, though for Rosemary it was just a passing thing—boys and clothes and schoolwork took precedence over bomb shelters and gathering stockpiles of supplies.

Rob's obsession grew and grew until it drove a wedge between them. Rosemary saw the same strange glimmer in his eyes that their father had when he used to lecture them about rationing or where to go if the bombs started dropping and they weren't close to home.

He'd changed. He was no longer the fun-loving big brother who beat up Steve Grasso for poking her in the boob or begrudgingly took her to see *Snow White* at the Kendall Theater. Self-preservation became his only concern. Survival at all costs. She got tired of defending him to other people, of fighting with him because she didn't share his bleak outlook for the future.

They hadn't seen each other since their mother's funeral. Without her around, there was no reason to keep up the appearance of being a loving family. Rosemary had wept many nights over it, but what was done was done. Seeing her brother would only open the old wounds that had never properly healed when their father left.

She always figured it would take a catastrophe to bring them back together.

She'd been right.

"I'll be right back. Feel free to look around," he said, hustling down one of the old buses to make his call. She wondered what kind of people he knew. Were they other paranoid mole people? How could they possibly help?

She walked down one of the corridors. It was lined with folding tables—jugs of water on one, old board games on another, unmarked cardboard boxes everywhere. He'd installed low-wattage bulbs in the ceiling. It gave just enough light to see things clearly, but also created sharp shadows and dark, foreboding corners. Rosemary could feel the weight of the earth pressing down on her.

*I hope he reinforced the hell out of these buses*, she thought, walking back and down another corridor. She couldn't get over how quiet it was here. It truly was like being buried alive.

Now this corridor, this is the one that would get him on an FBI watch list. It was stacked from floor to ceiling with guns of every make and model. He had enough here to outfit an army. He used to tell her that when the dust settled, if the damn Ruskies dared to claim the land for their own, he'd be there to plant them.

This is exactly why she'd come to Rob.

Her fingers were gliding down the cold barrel of a rifle when her brother came up behind her and said, "I got that from a German guy out of Sarasota. I don't know where he got fifty of them, but I was glad to take them off his hands."

"Where did you get the money to buy all this stuff?" She couldn't believe how much his armory had grown. It must have cost a fortune.

"I have my ways. Your big bro is pretty damn smart when he's not sitting on his brain."

Rosemary chuckled.

"I've got good news. I called a guy I know down in the Carolinas. He's a former government employee from a place with some familiar initials. He got me the address for AdventureCo, no problem. But there's a catch."

Rosemary's heart skipped a beat.

"Go on." She didn't care what the catch was. Once she got that address, nothing and no one was going to stop her.

"He said that AdventureCo has been a company of interest for years. There's some pretty strange shit going on there, but so far they've been allowed to operate under the radar. We're talking some bad hombres. So bad, even the big guns don't wanna fuck with them."

Rosemary picked up an assault rifle, found a magazine, and slammed it home. It was amazing how the lessons he'd taught her in the beginning, when she thought his hobby was cool, all came back to her. "I don't care if AdventureCo is run by the ghosts of Stalin and Hitler. I'm going down there to get my family back. I came here to see if you could lend me some guns. Now that you have an address, I just want to get on the road before it's too late."

He handed her a folded piece of paper. Before she could grab it, he pulled it back.

"Oh, there is a condition."

"What?" she said, feeling as if her flesh was crawling with fire ants. She wanted to be on the road, pushing the speed limit, headed south.

"I'm coming with you."

"Rob, no. This is my family. I'll handle it."

"I know you will. You're one tough broad. But you're going to need someone at your back. This place spooked my contact, and he's been in two wars. Besides, your son is my family, too. I wanna meet him."

She knew there was no sense arguing. And truth be told, she was happy to have him by her side.

He grabbed several large canvas bags from under a table. "Now, let's start packing."

# Chapter Ten

The drive to South Carolina would be long, but the act of being in motion made Rosemary feel as if they were making some headway. Flying would have been faster and easier, but she was pretty sure no airline would allow them to carry their arsenal onto the plane. Rob had covered the three full bags with a piece of wood that had fabric stapled onto it so that it looked, at least from a distance, like the bottom of her trunk. He then piled the usual detritus that accumulates in a car on top of that, just to cover their asses should they get stopped and some overenthusiastic state trooper decided to comb through the car.

Despite not seeing each other for over ten years, Rosemary and Rob spoke very little. Somewhere around Virginia, he asked, "Did the man on the phone say they had taken your husband and son to South Carolina?"

Gripping the wheel, eyes narrowed into slits, she said, "No, not in so many words."

"So there's a chance they might not be there at all."

"No."

"What makes you so sure?"

She swerved around a slow-moving car in the left lane, cutting in front of the Buick so close, they nearly clipped bumpers. A horn blared and she saw the woman behind the wheel give her the finger.

"Call it mother's intuition. Besides, it seems like they've carved out a nice little hideout for themselves down in Tegan's Mill. Where else would they run and hide where they'd be so protected?"

Rob rolled the window down, lit up a cigarette, and took a long, slow drag.

"Give me one," she said.

He lit it before handing it over to her. She inhaled. Her lungs burned and she coughed a bit. When she inhaled again, it felt like heaven. Her body tingled as smoke filled the car.

*Just like riding a bike*, she thought.

"You sure you don't want to pull over and call the cops?" he asked.

She glanced at him as if he'd asked her to strangle Mother Theresa on live TV. "You know I can't."

Rob closed his eyes and nodded. "Just checking. We don't need them. I want to make sure you haven't changed your mind."

They might not need the police, but it would be nice to have some forces on their side. If this AdventureCo was big enough to command the silence of the mayor, what could Rosemary and Rob possibly do to them?

"Take them by surprise and piss in their Cheerios," she mumbled, sucking the final embers of the cigarette and tossing the butt out the window onto I-95.

"What did you say?"

"Nothing. Just thinking out loud."

* * * *

They stopped for gas in North Carolina. Rob suggested they go to the diner across the street and grab some grub.

Rosemary had unfolded the map Rob had brought along—it turned out he had drawers of maps, of not just the entire United States but every developed country in the world—and estimated how much driving time until they'd hit Tegan's Mill.

"It's just another four hours or so," she said, eager to get back on the road.

"All the more reason to fortify ourselves while we can. You never send an army onto the battlefield on an empty stomach. Even if you're not hungry, force yourself to eat. You'll be thankful for it later."

Kathy's Diner had two long counters and ten booths along the windows, all with a lovely view of the gas station and entrance ramp to the highway. The overwhelming scent of coffee and grease set Rosemary's stomach to grumbling. She couldn't remember the last time she'd eaten. It might have been the night before.

The waitress, a young pregnant girl with a faded name tag that said Katie showed them to a booth. The menus were encased with crackling plastic that left her fingers sticky.

"Don't order anything crazy like ravioli or scrod," Rob said, grinning. When they were growing up, Rosemary ordered ravioli every time they went to a diner, and it was always terrible. "Stick to what a greasy spoon like this knows best. And no salads. Those are nothing but empty calories."

She was suddenly so hungry, there was no way in hell she'd waste it on a salad. She had a patty melt with fries, coleslaw, three pickles, and a chocolate shake. By the time she was done, her stomach was bloated. It was the best damn meal she'd ever had.

A wave of guilt washed over her. How could she have enjoyed a meal when Dwight and Gavin were God knows where? Were they being fed, or did the creeps at AdventureCo lock them up and starve them? Before she knew it, tears were cascading down her cheeks.

Rob put his cigarette out in the remaining french fries on his plate and moved over to sit next to her.

"I know, I know. We're going to get them back."

"Can we go now?" she asked, sniffling. If she didn't get in the car right now, she felt like she would lose her mind.

"Yeah, come on." He left a ten on the table and walked her out of the diner.

She spotted a phone booth and decided to make a quick detour. "I just want to call home, see if anyone answers."

Maybe they'd never been taken far and returned just after she'd left. Or Gavin had found a way to escape and was at this very moment with Dwight on their couch wondering if she'd been abducted as well.

The phone rang six times, and then the answering machine picked up.

"No luck?" Rob asked, leaning against the booth, a toothpick in his mouth.

"No, but I can retrieve my messages over the phone. Hold on." She dialed the five-digit code and waited.

"You have one new message."

Her heart galloped.

*Please be Gavin or Dwight. Please.*

"Hello, bitch. You have any more complaints you'd like to file? Oh, that's right, you can't, can you? Unlike our money back guarantee, there is no policy on getting people back. We apologize for the inconvenience." The insane laughter that followed drove Rosemary to the brink.

"Shut the fuck up!" she shouted, slamming the phone down again and again until it shattered into sharp pieces. Her brother pulled her out of the booth. Several people who had driven up to the diner were outside of their cars staring at them.

Rosemary couldn't stop trembling. She fumbled for her car keys that had tumbled to the bottom of her purse, speed walking to the car.

"What happened, Rosemary?" Rob said, almost on her heels.

"We have to get there right away," she said, grinding her teeth so hard she saw stars. She gunned the engine, put the car in drive, and laid down half the rubber on her tires as she careened onto the ramp. "I'm going to kill every last one of them."

Rob grinned. "Now that's what I'm talking about."

# Chapter Eleven

If those crazy bastards from AdventureCo were still calling her, they'd begin to get suspicious if she didn't start answering the phone. Rosemary worried that they'd suspect she was with the police and make good on their threat.

She kept the speedometer pinned at eighty. Along the way, Rob gave her a tutorial on the various weapons he'd stocked for their mission. He'd gotten his hands on some primo shit (his words) since she'd last seen him, stuff from other countries that would blow a hole through a polar bear. It was all white noise to her right now. As far as she was concerned, there were big guns and little guns and they all had triggers that were easily pulled.

There wasn't a moment's hesitation wondering if she'd have the guts to shoot someone. They wanted to play rough. She was ready to play rougher. No one touched a hair on her child's head and got away with it. No one. She desperately wished Gavin were here with her now. No evil company could stand between united parents and their child.

Rob chain-smoked and talked strategy. If Gavin couldn't be here, she had to admit her brother was a damn good substitute. Perhaps even better, only because he was slightly crazy and heavily armed.

"You hearing me?" he said, tapping her upper arm.

She nodded, eyes on the road. "Yes. How much farther until the exit?"

He looked down at the map on his lap, his finger tracing the route he'd marked with a highlighter. "Let's see. We passed exit twenty-nine just back there, so it looks like ten miles. Once we jump off the highway it'll be another couple of miles on back roads."

Swallowing hard, she felt the rising patty melt burn her throat.

"We go in with silencers," Rob continued. "The quieter we can be, the better. No sense bringing the place down on our heads the moment we step inside. You got it?"

"Got it." The anxiety bubbling up inside of her had her nerves tingling. She willed the old car to go faster, but it started to shimmy alarmingly when she neared ninety.

"Part of stealth mode is not getting pulled over by South Carolina cops. Take it down a notch, sis. You want another coffin nail?"

"God yes." Kools had never been her smoke of choice, but beggars couldn't be choosers. The cigarette did little to calm her frayed nerves.

They took the long curving exit onto Route 35, which was just a two-lane road surrounded by red clay and shrubs.

"Go west," Rob said.

A quarter mile in, they took a right down a narrow, winding road, then a left that dumped them into an empty bowl of cleared land, sparse clumps of weeds growing between cracks in the concrete. It looked like a long-abandoned parking lot, but there were no vacant structures, no evidence of why this spot would have been paved at all.

It was a complete dead end. Rosemary made a U-turn and drove out of the bowl.

"Maybe we should have gone left," she said.

Rob's brows scrunched together. "No, according to the map, we need to go right."

"Well, you saw the same thing I did. There's nothing there," she said, unable to mask her agitation.

She wanted to roll down the window and scream, *"Dwight, Gavin, where are you? I'm here! I'm here!"*

Taking the road on the left brought them to a thick chain roped between two massive trees, a rusted NO TRESPASSING sign clamped to the middle of the chain.

"This looks more promising," Rosemary said.

"It might, but that's not it."

Rob had always been so sure of himself to the point of arrogance. Rosemary felt some of the old anger flare up.

She cast him a hard look and he shot back, "Hey, I know how to read a map and this isn't the place. It's back there by that lot."

"But there's nothing there."

"And there's nothing here."

"There's that." She pointed at the sign. "Seems to me AdventureCo is a place that doesn't want to be seen."

Rob tossed the map into the back seat. "Which is exactly why this isn't it. Doesn't that seem a little too obvious to you? Just do me a favor and circle back. Give me two minutes. If we don't find anything, we come back here, okay?"

As much as Rosemary wanted to tell him to stuff it, this was his area of expertise. Right now, she was strung tighter than a drumhead. She'd give him two minutes but nothing more.

Rob told her to park just outside the bowl, keeping the car hidden on the access road. He took a gun from the back of his waistband and jumped out of the car. "Stay here. I'll be right back."

"No, I'm coming with you."

He gave her a lopsided smile. "Recon is best done alone." He opened the trunk and came back with a handgun with a long silencer screwed onto the end. "Keep this handy, but please look before you shoot. I don't want to be fragged by friendly fire."

Running in a crouch, he disappeared before she could say anything. The gun was awfully heavy, the silencer upsetting the balance. Rosemary's head swiveled on her neck as she kept a close eye on every direction, expecting someone to jump out at any moment.

It wasn't a small concern that she would shoot her brother by mistake. She remembered to keep her finger on the trigger guard.

She sighed with relief when he came jogging back.

"I was right. Come on, let's unload the trunk."

She slung one of the heavy bags over her shoulder. Rob had one on each of his.

"Stay close to me," he said.

The vacant lot looked just as empty as before. A stray breeze kicked up some dust, forming a tiny cyclone that skittered past them.

"I don't see anything," she whispered.

"That's the whole point."

There was nowhere to hide, so they strode across the bowl.

Rosemary wondered what could possibly be out here. AdventureCo had to have a factory making their dangerous toys. How the hell could you hide a factory in an open lot?

Rob stopped and she bumped into him. He pointed to their left. "Right there. You've got to be up to some seriously bad shit for this kind of setup."

All she saw was the jagged stump of what was once a massive tree at the corner of the lot. The stump looked to be about ten feet high, the victim of a hurricane or lightning strike or something frightful cooked up by Mother Nature.

"A tree stump?"

He tugged her along. "Yeah, only it's not real."

When they got to it, he grabbed her hand and laid it flat against the stump. It was smooth and cold.

Like plastic.

"What?" she said.

Now he pulled her around to the back of the stump. He moved his hands along the fake bark, and one of the wedges slid aside, revealing a keyhole.

"This is too Alice in Wonderland for me," she said. "You mean to tell me we have to go through this stump and AdventureCo is down there?"

"Yep. Only this time, you're bringing the Mad Hatter with you." He took a square case from his pocket. She remembered it as the lock-picking kit he'd bought at a head shop when they were teens. Over the course of that summer, he'd taught himself how to open almost any lock. She worried then that he was turning into a thief.

*Maybe that's how he has the money to buy all the guns*, she thought. It didn't matter how he got them. Not now.

There was a faint click and a door opened up. Rob darted his head in and out quickly.

"Just like my place. There's a ladder leading down, but it's too dark for me to make out what's at the bottom."

Rosemary looked around. "You think they have cameras out here? They could be watching us right now." She didn't need to add that they could be walking into an ambush.

Rob took a deep breath, getting a flashlight from one of his bags. "I checked and didn't see any, but they could have one of those new tiny cameras anywhere. If you want, we could head back and get the police to raid the place."

She was pretty sure the police would deny there was anything out here, just like the mayor had. Plus, if AdventureCo could see what was going on up top, the moment they spied cop cars, Dwight and Gavin were doomed.

"No," she said. "Let's do this."

They headed down the rungs. The door closed on its own, shutting out the daylight. Rosemary said a silent prayer, especially for forgiveness, because if she was successful, she was going to have blood on her hands before the day was done.

# Chapter Twelve

The climb down was longer than the one to Rob's bunker. When they got to the bottom, motion sensors made a set of overhead lights snap on, startling them so much, they had their guns out and ready to blast the bulbs. They looked down a long hallway that looked like the interior of a typical office building, minus the doors leading to offices. There was a set of double doors at the end of the hall.

Rob kept his voice low, "Looks like there's only one way to go. I'll take point."

Rosemary's heart beat so hard, she thought it would crawl up her throat and sprint out of her mouth. She was sure her brother could hear it echoing in the bright hallway.

She pictured her family, focusing on them and not her fear, walking slowly and quietly behind Rob.

The doors had another lock. Rob took out his kit. "Watch our backs."

This lock was giving him a little more trouble. His breath hissed between his teeth.

*Where are the people?* Rosemary wondered. The place was too clean to be just a front. But it was so quiet.

"You know, I'm sorry it took something like this to see you again," Rob said, eyes squinted, working the picks with his calloused fingers.

"I'm sorry, too."

"I know you all think I lost my mind."

Rosemary smiled. "Yeah, well, maybe a little."

"Kind of a good thing I did, huh?"

She hefted the pistol in her hand.

"I guess it is."

She heard a soft pop, and he leaned his sweaty forehead on the door. "We're in." He stood up, slinging the bags back onto his shoulders. Holding up three fingers, he gave a silent countdown.

On three, he opened the door.

The blast was deafening.

Rosemary's face was splashed with something hot and terrible smelling, her ears ringing.

She looked in horror at where her brother's head had been just a second before. Blood spurted from the interior of his exposed neck for just a moment before his body hit the ground.

\* \* \* \*

Without thinking, Rosemary raised her gun and fired blindly, pulling the trigger over and over until the gun was empty, the silenced shots making *whup, whup* sounds as they burst from the barrel. Her body jolted with each depression of the trigger, expecting return fire to do to her what had been done to Rob.

Legs trembling, she was shocked to see two men face down on the floor, blood pooling around them. They wore black suits and shiny dress shoes. Somehow, she'd managed to hit them both in the chest, the exit wounds ruining their suit jackets.

There was no one else around, but that wouldn't last long. The men didn't use silencers, their shots loud enough to wake the dead. Kneeling by Rob's cooling body, Rosemary fumbled in her bag for a fresh clip. She found four, jamming the other three in her waistband.

She couldn't bring herself to touch Rob, her tears falling on his bloody shoulder. Turning away, she saw the splattered remains of his head on the wall and floor. She threw up so hard she thought she felt a rib crack. Wiping her mouth with the back of her hand, she willed her legs to move. She had two choices: the long corridor leading to her left or the one leading to her right. Again, there were no doors.

There was no way she could walk past the mess of her brother's head, so she chose the right, stepping over the fallen men. Rob had talked about stealth, but that ship had sailed. She ran as fast as she could, breathing heavily. There was a thick, steel door at the end of this one. Lock picking was not one of her skill sets.

Looking in the bag, she wrapped her hands around one of the things she'd managed to listen to Rob explain about during the drive, what was to be used when shit went south.

Hoping not to be hit by a ricocheting bullet, she fired at the lock in the door until it popped open. Once it did, she pulled the pin on the flash-bang grenade and chucked it through the opening and closed her eyes.

Whoever was on the other side would be blinded and disoriented. Wasting no time, she stepped inside and saw three men, also in suits, staggering. She quickly shot them each in the head.

Just like smoking, firing a weapon was like riding a bike. She'd always been a good shot.

Through one man's blood smear on the window behind him, Rosemary saw that she had truly arrived, and it took her breath away.

# Chapter Thirteen

She looked out at the tremendous underground factory. Machines and conveyor belts pushed out novelty product after novelty product. There were rockets made of balsa wood and rubber bands, X-ray specs with red and white swirls on the lenses, giant ghosts that were nothing but cheap sheets, little plastic tanks that would one day hold disappointing sea serpents, and thinly pressed soldiers, tanks, and planes that would upset every little boy who bought them.

And there, just below her, was the big cardboard-cutting machine, spitting out nuclear sub after nuclear sub.

The hum of the machinery thrummed from her feet to her teeth. The factory was inordinately busy, meeting the demand of children everywhere who craved the wonders advertised in their comic books.

Except there were no people running the machines.

Using her sleeve, she wiped most of the blood away so there was no square inch of the factory floor hidden from her. It all ran by itself. She knew that robotics had come a long way and had taken over a ton of manual tasks, but didn't they still need people to run them and make sure things went according to plan?

The little room overlooking the factory was another dead end.

Red lights popped from the ceiling and flashed, a siren going off. Rosemary jumped, pulling the trigger and firing into the glass. It shattered with an ear-splitting crash, shards cascading over the equipment below. Someone burst through the door behind her. She swiveled around and fired, catching the man in the mouth, his teeth flying so hard, they buried themselves in the wall. His body slumped against the door, shutting it. It vibrated as someone slammed into it from the other side. The door didn't move, held fast by the dead weight.

"Shit, shit, shit."

There was only one way to go. She poked her head through the broken viewing window and looked down. Just seven feet below her was a metal gangway. Tossing the heavy bag over first, she leaped over the sill, landing on her feet, a sharp pain rocketing from her ankles to her knees and hips.

There was shouting above as more men worked to get the door open.

She was going to need a bigger gun. She took an assault rifle out of the bag. To test it, she fired at the nuclear sub machine. Bright sparks flew upward as metal clanked and stopped.

"Where the hell is my family?"

She worried that this was all there was and the Dwight and Gavin had been taken somewhere else. Running down the gangway, she shot at each machine, shattering the mechanisms that spewed out their crappy, dangerous merchandise.

"There!" someone shouted.

She glanced up. Several men had gotten through and spotted her. They raised their guns and fired. Rosemary catapulted off the gangway and rolled behind one of the big machines. The bullets from their pistols impotently bounced off it.

Taking a chance, she returned fire with the rifle, catching one man in the chest, nearly slicing him in half. He didn't even have time to scream before falling onto the factory floor.

A hail of bullets rained down on the machine. Rosemary pressed her back to it, riding it out.

*I can't stay here. They know where am I and they'll eventually box me in.*

She looked inside the bag. There were more flash-bang grenades. It would be an awfully long throw to get it through that window. But maybe she didn't need to get it that far. Just close enough to blind them.

Darting out from behind the machine, she spit a line of fire. The men ducked, giving her time to pull the pin and hurl the grenade as far as she could. It landed on the gangway she'd initially dropped down onto.

The men, not hearing it, poked their heads back, guns drawn.

Rosemary ducked for cover. There was an incredible explosion this time, the bass of it so heavy and deep, it made her heart skip several beats. The factory shuddered from the impact.

That wasn't a flash-bang.

There was a hole in the wall where the grenade had landed. The men were nowhere to be seen. Shrapnel had flown in every direction.

"Holy crap."

She realized she couldn't carry the full-on grenades in the bag with people shooting at her. If a stray bullet hit one of them, she'd be vaporized.

There were four in all. She wished she'd been able to take Rob's bags. She could only imagine what he had in them. She pulled the pins and launched each grenade at different production areas of the factory. Heavy machinery became scrap metal, novelty toys blown to smithereens.

Making her way to the factory floor, Rosemary spied an open door at the other end. Fires had broken out everywhere. The conveyor belts had all stopped. Black smoke roiled in the vast room. The smell of burning plastic and other toxic chemicals burned her nose and lungs.

Churning her legs as fast as she could, Rosemary headed for the door, expecting an army of AdventureCo security to be waiting for her. That was fine by her. She was ready for them. Nothing was going to stop her. Not until she found her family. The rifle was in one hand, the pistol in the other.

Sprinting through the door, she fired in both directions.

The dazzling white corridor was devoid of people. Oily smoke billowed into it behind her.

To her left was something that looked like an altar. Made of marble, the base had carvings of naked people writhing in a tight mass, agony etched onto the faces of the men, women, and children. A black cloth had been laid over the altar, and there was a chipped, wooden bowl in the center. Rosemary inched closer to the altar, wary of anyone following her into the corridor.

Standing beside it, she looked into the bowl.

It was filled with blood, or something that looked an awful lot like blood. She poked the bowl with her gun. Something floated to the top.

It was an ear.

She gasped, stumbling back and almost tripping over her own feet.

In that brief glance, she saw the tiny notch in the outer fold of the ear, as if someone had pressed their nail into it and left a lasting impression.

It was Dwight's.

# Chapter Fourteen

Rosemary roared with rage, shooting the altar, defacing the intricate carving and blowing the bowl to tiny pieces. What kind of sickness was this? Just what the fuck was AdventureCo? It was no wonder the mayor refused to talk about it. Something this evil had long-reaching tendrils. If she wasn't so goddamned mad right now, she'd be paralyzed by fear.

She had to move fast. It felt as if the walls were closing in around her, as if time were spinning out of control.

They wanted her to find that ear.

All along, she thought she was taking them by surprise, and in reality, they'd been leading her here.

At least that's how it felt.

She had to crouch to get under the smoke, hustling in the other direction, searching for a door, any door, that could lead her closer to her family... if they were still alive.

She heard and then felt a bullet whiz past her ear. She fired back into the growing gloom. Still running, she could see just enough to step over the body, legs in spasm as death took hold.

"Come on, come on. Where's a fucking door?"

Just as she said it, a door swung open at the end of the corridor. Three men emerged, each armed with a rifle. Rosemary dropped to the ground, their bullets sizzling overhead. Knees propped on the floor, she opened fire into the crowd of men. One by one they collapsed, grabbing their legs. She kept shooting, making sure to get them in the torso and head as they sank to her level.

Collecting herself, she made it to the doorway and pressed her back to the wall, waiting to see if anyone else was coming. She wished she'd saved one of the grenades. She could just launch it and walk in after it had cleared the way.

*It could also kill Dwight and Gavin if they're close by*, she thought.

Unlike before, she stepped through this door without shooting. She felt she was getting deeper into the AdventureCo maze, which meant she was getting closer to her family. She'd have to be very careful from here on.

Instead of another long hallway, this led to a huge, dark room. A red light from someplace she couldn't see cast an eerie glow. The room, as far as she could tell, was empty. The walls here weren't fabricated. No, they were rough and rocky, carved from the earth itself.

The sound of clapping caught her breath in her throat.

A man came out of the darkness just twenty feet in front of her. He too wore a suit, his black hair parted to one side, a shit-eating grin on his face.

"Not bad," he said in a gravelly voice, "for a dumb whore."

She knew that voice. He was the one who had been calling her, tormenting her, the one who had taken her son and husband!

He continued to clap, the sound echoing in the vast room.

Rosemary fired the rifle in a steady line that riddled him with bullets from his crotch to the top of his head. The smile shredded like bloody cheese. Each half of his body fell in opposite directions.

"I'm not a dumb whore," she growled.

"No, you're apparently not," another voice, this one smoother than silk, replied.

She couldn't see who had spoken, but he was somewhere in the darkness ahead of her.

She raised the rifle.

"I wouldn't do that if I were you."

"It's a good thing you're not me," Rosemary said. "Now where are my son and husband?"

"Mom!"

Hearing Dwight's voice almost brought her to her knees. The rifle felt like a ten-ton weight.

"Dwight!"

Their voices bounced around the room, making it impossible to tell which direction they'd come from.

Rosemary put the rifle down. It hung from a strap around her shoulder.

"The pistol too, if you please," the silky voice said.

It clattered to the floor, along with the bag.

Exhaustion flooded her muscles, tunneling through her bones. She just wanted to hold Dwight and fall asleep.

"I thank you."

"For what? Give me back my family."

"For a wonderful afternoon. You can't know how much pleasure you've given me. Such anger, such determination. I'm not ashamed to admit you've made me quite erect."

What kind of sick bastard was this? Rosemary felt her stomach heave.

"Why don't you show yourself?" she said. "Only cowards hide in the shadows. Only little men prey on children."

Someone grunted. A red spotlight snapped on. Gavin was curled in a ball. She ran to him.

"Oh my God, Gavin, are you all right?"

Her husband's skin was cold and clammy. He looked up at her with wide, terrified eyes. His mouth trembled, but he couldn't speak.

"What have you done to him?" she shouted.

There was a long, painful silence, then, "He wanted to see what kind of a man had done this to his family, just like you. So, I let him see."

Rosemary's flesh felt as if it wanted to crawl off her bones. She couldn't explain why. Gavin was in shock, of that there was no doubt. She helped him to his feet. He clung to her like an infant.

"Now give me back my son."

"The fire burns deep in you." He made a low, soft moaning sound that set her teeth on edge. "I could just drink you up."

"Mommy?"

Dwight shuffled from the darkness, a blindfold wrapped around his eyes. Still propping her husband up, she rushed to meet him, clutching him to her body. She kissed the top of his head again and again, weeping uncontrollably. With one hand, she undid the knot of the blindfold and let it drop to the floor. She felt the side of his head, letting out a sharp cry when she saw that he had both of his ears.

"It was just a slight enticement to, ah, stoke the flames," the voice said.

"You came for us," Dwight said, crying into her chest.

"Of course I did, baby. I'd never let anyone hurt you."

Gavin gripped her shoulder, shaking like a leaf.

Dwight said, "I want to go home."

"I know, honey. I know."

The only problem was, the way out was on fire. Rosemary hadn't seen any other means of exiting the underground lair.

"Let us out," Rosemary said.

Silence was her reply.

"If what you say is true, we both got what we wanted. Show me how to get the hell out of here."

This time, the voice chuckled.

"Yes, it seems your use is at an end. You're not the first, you know. Oh, but you've been the best. Yes, by far, the best."

A bright light spilled into the room as a door opened on the other side. Rosemary and Dwight shielded their eyes. They walked as one toward the light. The voice remained silent as they trudged across the room, the acrid smell of smoke following them.

Before they stepped out of the room, Rosemary said, "Who are you? What did all of this mean?"

"Oh, I think you know who I am. Care to see for yourself? I promise, it's not something you'll ever forget."

Gavin stumbled away from her, falling across the threshold. Scrabbling on his hands and knees, he crawled into the fresh air and light, casting furtive glances back, blubbering incoherently.

Rosemary turned to see what he was looking at.

Dwight tugged hard on her arm. "Don't, Mom."

She looked to her son, the distraught shell of her husband.

"He wanted to see what kind of a man had done this to his family. So, I let him see," the voice said.

The ground rumbled and there was a loud bass pop, as if something exceedingly heavy had dropped from above. Rosemary instinctively shielded her son. Gavin curled up into a ball, his hair coated with dirt as his mouth opened and closed silently, like a fish.

She turned back and saw nothing but the clear, vacant lot. The chamber they had emerged from was gone, as if it had never been there at all. Even the stump that had been the secret entrance to AdventureCo's underground lair was missing, replaced by scrub grass.

*Rob's down there*, she thought. *He'll be down there forever.* Her heart ached for a brother she thought she'd never see again.

It took a lot of gentle coaxing to get Gavin back on his feet. She wasn't even sure he recognized her. But he did listen to her, taking her hand and following her to the car.

Dwight stayed glued to her side, sniffling.

"The man told me that you would come," he said.

She stopped, looking down at his tired face, his eyes bloodshot and glassy. "He was right."

He looked behind them at the field of nothing. "He said if you did, it would be bad for you. That he would see you again. What did he mean?"

Cupping his face in her hands, she kissed his forehead. Gavin stared at the ground, arms slack, completely disconnected from reality.

Rosemary shivered in the southern heat, hoping Dwight didn't notice. She put on the best smile she could muster and held on to the hands of her son and husband. "Let's go home."

She helped Gavin lie down in the back of the car. She buckled Dwight in the passenger seat.

When she went to slide behind the wheel, she found something tucked into the seat.

It was a five-dollar bill.

Don't Miss *Jurassic, Florida*
the first book in Hunter Shea's One Size Eats All series!

## Florida. It's Where You Go To Die.

Welcome to Polo Springs, a sleepy little town on Florida's Gulf Coast. It's a great place to live—if you don't mind the hurricanes. Or the flooding. Or the unusual wildlife…

## Iguanas. They're Everywhere.

Maybe it's the weather. But the whole town is overrun with the little green bastards this year. They're causing a lot of damage. They're eating everything in sight. And they're just the babies…

## Humans. They're What's For Dinner.

The mayor wants to address the iguana problem. But when Hurricane Ramona slams the coast, the town has a bigger problem on their hands. Bigger iguanas. Bigger than a double-wide. Unleashed by the storm, this razor-toothed horde of prehistoric predators rises up from the depths— and descends on the town like retirees at an early bird special. Except humans are on the menu. And it's all you can eat…

# About the Author

**Hunter Shea** is the product of a misspent childhood watching scary movies, reading forbidden books, and wishing Bigfoot would walk past his house. He doesn't just write about the paranormal—he actively seeks out the things that scare the hell out of people and experiences them for himself. Hunter's novels can even be found on display at the International Cryptozoology Museum. The Montauk Monster was named one of the best reads of the summer by Publishers Weekly. Not since Dr. Frankenstein has anyone been so dedicated to making monsters. Hunter Shea has penned such titles as The Jersey Devil, Tortures of the Damned, They Rise, Swamp Monster Massacre and The Dover Demon. Living with his wonderful family and two cats, he's happy to be close enough to New York City to gobble down Gray's Papaya hot dogs when the craving hits. You can follow his madness at www.huntershea.com.

Printed in the United States
by Baker & Taylor Publisher Services